"You forgot to leave a shoe behind when you left the party, Cinderella."

Courtney leaned back in her library chair and sighed. "What are you doing here, Denver?"

"I told you I'd be seeing you again. You should have believed me."

Stalling for time, she reached for her cup of coffee and took a sip, uncomfortably aware that he was watching every move she made.

She set the cup down and poured more coffee into it. "I only have the one cup, but you can share it if you'd like some."

He took the cup from her. Instead of drinking from the side closest to him, he turned the cup and drank from the same place her lips had been. It was a strangely intimate gesture that had her breath shuddering in her chest.

When she slowly raised her gaze from his mouth, she felt her heartbeat quicken at the heat radiating from his eyes. "No," she murmured, as though he had asked her a question.

The lines at the corners of his eyes deepened as he smiled. "Yes. You can run all you want, Courtney, but I'll catch you eventually. . . ."

WHAT ARE *LOVESWEPT* ROMANCES?

They are stories of true romance and touching emotion. We believe those two very important ingredients are constants in our highly sensual and very believable stories in the *LOVESWEPT* line. Our goal is to give you, the reader, stories of consistently high quality that may sometimes make you laugh, sometimes make you cry, but are always fresh and creative and contain many delightful surprises within their pages.

Most romance fans read an enormous number of books. Those they truly love, they keep. Others may be traded with friends and soon forgotten. We hope that each *LOVESWEPT* romance will be a treasure—a "keeper." We will always try to publish

LOVE STORIES YOU'LL NEVER FORGET
BY AUTHORS YOU'LL ALWAYS REMEMBER

The Editors

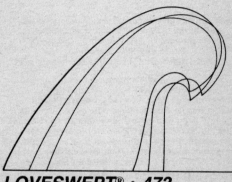

LOVESWEPT® • 473
Patt Bucheister
Hot Pursuit

 BANTAM BOOKS
NEW YORK • TORONTO • LONDON • SYDNEY • AUCKLAND

HOT PURSUIT

A Bantam Book / May 1991

*If you would be interested in receiving protective vinyl
covers for your Loveswept books, please write to this address
for information:*

> Loveswept
> Bantam Books
> P.O. Box 985
> Hicksville, NY 11802

ISBN 0-553-44077-2

Published simultaneously in the United States and Canada

PRINTED IN THE UNITED STATES OF AMERICA

OPM   0 9 8 7 6 5 4 3 2 1

One

On a scale of one to ten this party was a five, Courtney Caine thought as she leaned against the wall of the large living room. She'd been to some that were worse and a few that were better.

The house had been redecorated since she'd last been there, about six months ago. The impressive colonial-style mansion, which belonged to her mother's manager, had been overhauled more times than her housekeeper's eight-year-old station wagon, Courtney thought with amusement. When Tyrell Gilbert had bought the house on the James River in Virginia ten years ago, her mother had thought he was nuts. It was so far away from his office in Nashville, she'd told him, and some distance from an airport. Those advantages, to Tyrell, had been the main attractions. Now her mother had recently purchased a similar piece of property outside of Yorktown for the same reasons.

Courtney scanned the room. She preferred to be

an observer, watching festivities from a distance instead of mingling with the people standing around in clusters. She wasn't in the mood to make polite chitchat, or to answer questions about her limp.

Someone always noticed her limp and inquired about it, nicely but persistently. She limped no worse than someone who had a blister on his foot, yet it drew more questions than she liked. Her answers depended on her mood and the way the inquiry was made, and they ranged from the ridiculous to the sublime, from an injury while skiing to stepping on a nail. Anything but the truth. She had worn a brace on her leg for most of her life and was used to it. But no matter how hard she tried, she had never become accustomed to the way some people looked at her pityingly when they learned the truth, or the way she was treated once they saw the brace. It was easier to attempt to minimize the exposure than draw attention to it.

Since she was wearing a long dress that night, the brace below her left knee wasn't visible. As long as she stayed where she was, detailed explanations about her favoring her leg weren't necessary.

She noticed a photographer with two cameras dangling around his neck scouting the room for the guest of honor. Courtney was adept at avoiding cameras whenever she was with her famous family. There were few recognizable photos of her face, which was the way she wanted it. Unlike her mother and sisters, she would rather be in a library crowded with books than at a party stuffed with people, or on a stage in front of an audience crammed with music fans.

In another hour she would have fulfilled the bargain she'd made with her mother, after surviving several hours of gentle but persistent nagging from her. The corporate world could use an expert negotiator like Amethyst Rand, Courtney thought with amusement. Her mother knew she didn't like to appear at the public functions that were part of her family's life as entertainment figures—especially for the last two years. Amethyst usually accepted Courtney's refusals good-naturedly, except when it was important to her to have all her girls together. Like tonight. Amethyst was the guest of honor at a party given by her manager to celebrate her twenty-five years in the country-western music business.

From her position against the wall nearest the entrance to the living room, Courtney could see through an arched doorway a long buffet table in the dining room. She didn't have to stroll around the damask-covered table to know what type of food was laid out. There would be caviar in ice-lined bowls, pâté arranged in the shape of a fish or some other unlikely creature, stuffed shrimp, and other exotic edibles chosen for their cost and displayed so beautifully, it was a shame to disturb any of them. After two hours the elaborate arrangement of food had barely been touched by the elegantly dressed guests. The same couldn't be said for the champagne. The supply had been dwindling at a steady pace.

Courtney couldn't help smiling at the thought that the guest of honor would rather have hot dogs, potato chips, and a cool glass of lemonade or a beer, rather than all the costly, fancy foods.

Privately her mother called this kind of food "nib-blins," pretty to look at but not what she would want to live on.

Courtney's smile faded when she realized she was being watched. Again. Even before she looked around, she knew who was staring at her. No one else in the room created that strange prickling sensation along her skin as when one particular man looked at her. He didn't simply look at her. His stare ate her up with an intensity unlike anything she'd ever experienced.

He was standing just inside the doorway leading to the dining room, gazing directly at her, as he had several times during the evening. Even with the length of the living room and all those people between them, she could feel the impact of his disturbing scrutiny.

Like the other men present, he wore a tuxedo. He seemed completely at ease in the formal attire, unlike some of the other men, who stood stiffly for fear of wrinkling themselves or tugged at their tight collars. His hair was thick, straight, and black, worn a little bit long, and she got the impression he was the type of man who didn't particularly care about current styles or fashion. His skin was tanned, his eyes bold as he watched her.

When she'd first seen him, she had thought he resembled the solitary Indian on horseback in the painting in her mother's home in Nashville. He had the same high cheekbones, chiseled nose, and dark eyes that saw into the soul.

He was certainly trying to see into hers, she thought uneasily. Refusing to be intimidated by his frank stare, she looked back at him defiantly. A corner of his mouth curved upward slightly as he acknowledged the challenge in her eyes.

She didn't know who he was, but she did know who he had arrived with. Breaking away from his compelling gaze, she searched the room for the woman he should be paying some attention to. Her sister, Amber. At first she didn't see Amber anywhere among the crush of people. Then she caught a glimpse of her making her way through the crowd toward the dark-haired stranger. Courtney smiled. In a minute he would be too occupied by the red-haired dynamo to have time to stare at her any longer.

Amber was the youngest of the three girls and most like their mother. She was cheerful, funny, and a good sport about everything except being ignored. Crystal was the oldest. She was more dedicated to her career than Amber, and somewhat cynical about life in general and men in particular. All three sisters had different fathers, but were intensely loyal to one another and to their mother.

Which was why Courtney was irritated with the man who was staring at her instead of paying attention to her sister.

For the last five years both of Courtney's sisters had been singing professionally and were as comfortable in crowds as their irrepressible mother. The three of them were nicknamed the Jewels of the South and were popular with several generations of country-western music fans. Amethyst usually recorded and appeared on stage alone, while Crystal and Amber performed as a duet.

Several times a year they would all appear together. Courtney was proud of them—and loved them, and she felt no envy or desire to exchange her academic life for theirs.

She shook her head when a waiter approached her with a silver tray containing long-stemmed glasses full of bubbling wine. She was still holding the glass she'd picked up when she'd arrived two hours earlier. By now the champagne was warm and flat. It didn't matter, since she didn't plan on drinking it. The glass was a prop, as was the faint smile shaping her mouth.

She watched with amusement as Amber led her escort to the buffet table. As usual Amber was talking a mile a minute. Courtney almost felt sorry for the man as she caught his rather dazed expression. Her sister's conversation could bounce around from subject to subject like a ricocheting Ping-Pong ball, unconcerned with its final destination.

"Have you had a chance to see Tyrell's newly redecorated powder room?" a woman asked her.

Courtney turned her head to look at Crystal, who had suddenly appeared beside her. "No," she said, smiling broadly. Comparing people's tastes in bathrooms was a game they'd played since they were children. "What's it like?"

"Think cotton candy, Momma's old Cadillac, and Mavis Cravet's strapless wedding dress."

"It's pink?"

Chuckling, Crystal leaned back against the wall. "With little white flowers. Even the sink and the john. Remember the bathroom we saw at that party a couple of years ago in Richmond? At least

Tyrell's doesn't have mirrored ceilings and a chandelier."

Placing her barely touched glass of champagne on the tray of a passing waiter, Courtney said, "Or his divorce papers framed on the wall like that record producer in California you told me about." She let her gaze roam around the room. "Where is our host? I haven't seen Tyrell since I arrived."

"The last time I saw him, he was dragging Momma off to meet some guy from New York. You know Tyrell. He never misses a chance to promote Momma. Have you been able to talk to her at all tonight?"

Courtney smiled. "She caught me in the kitchen earlier."

"Did she tell you about the Mallory plantation?"

"Yes. I promised to find out all I can about the history of the place." She laughed softly. "I think it's the first time she realized having a history teacher for a daughter might come in handy."

"She's excited about living on a plantation. She's even looked up some recipes for mint julep."

"I hope it turns out better than that plantation punch she made at Christmas. It almost dissolved the fillings in my teeth."

As she turned to smile at her sister, Courtney saw Amber's escort staring at her again. He was standing about ten feet away in a group of several men, his gaze on her rather than the man who was talking. Amber was no longer at his side. She saw him look from her to Crystal, apparently comparing the two of them. It was easy for Courtney to guess what he was thinking, for the difference between her sister and herself was as marked as night and day. Crystal was all glittery and bright, from the beading on her soft yellow dress to her light blond hair piled on top of her head in a complicated style. Her makeup had been expertly applied, emphasizing her eyes, which were a darker shade of brown than Courtney's.

Courtney's dress had a tight white lace bodice and a long, flowing white skirt. Her ash blond hair was pulled back and fastened with a white velvet bow at the base of her neck. She'd applied her makeup lightly. She was understated simplicity beside her sister's explosion of light and elegance.

"I wonder," Crystal murmured, following the direction of Courtney's gaze, "what his bathroom looks like."

Courtney choked back a laugh. "Maybe you should ask Amber. She came with him."

"She only met him yesterday. He treats her like she's an amusing kid sister."

Courtney grinned. "Kind of like we do. What happened to the football player she was dating?"

"I gather he tried to make one pass too many."

Courtney groaned at the pun. "I noticed you came with the accountant. I thought you said he was boring."

"At least I have an escort, even if it's only boring Bruce. You, as usual, came alone."

"Don't start," Courtney warned. She hadn't dated in over two years, not since Philip Seavors had taught her a lesson about men she wasn't likely to forget for a long time.

Crystal sighed. "All right. I'll drop it." She again glanced at the dark-haired man. "Things are looking up. He hasn't taken his eyes off you for the last five minutes."

"He came with Amber." Courtney hesitated, then asked the question that had been on her mind since she'd first seen the man. "Who is he?"

"He's the man who's going to do the renovations on the plantation Momma just bought. She calls him Denver, which could either be his first name, his last name, or where he was born."

Courtney smiled. If their mother didn't think someone's name fit, she immediately renamed him or her with something she felt more appropriate.

Courtney's gaze was caught by Amethyst, who was standing next to the white piano on the far side of the living room, Amber at her side. Not for the first time Courtney thought of how the blond-haired Amethyst looked more like their sister than a woman old enough to be their mother. The sapphire blue gown she wore hugged her slender figure, and the matching high-heeled sandals added inches to her diminutive height. What nature hadn't supplied, expertly applied cosmetics did. This was her professional appearance, Courtney knew, honed over the years by experience. Her long painted nails and lashes might be fake, but her sense of humor and devotion to her family was very real.

Amethyst was wiggling her fingers in a summoning gesture, and Courtney turned to her sister.

"You're being summoned, Crys. It's show time."

Instead of strolling away, Crystal stepped directly in front of Courtney, her back to the people in the room. "Why don't you sing with us? You know it would mean a lot to Momma."

Courtney shook her head. "I don't want to lose my amateur standing."

"Come on. You used to sing with us at these type of things. Before that jerk Philip came along, you used to do a lot of things you no longer do."

"Crystal," Courtney warned again.

"I know. You don't want to talk about him."

Courtney was aware of the low rumble of conversation subsiding as the guests realized they were about to be entertained by Amethyst and her daughters. She could hear the piano player running his fingers over the keys. The last thing she wanted was to draw attention to herself by being the reason for Crystal's delay in joining Amethyst and Amber.

She raised her hand to her sister's arm. "You'd better go over there. The natives are getting restless."

Crystal shrugged and gave up.

A small scattering of applause accompanied her as she walked across the Oriental carpet to her mother and sister. All the attention was now on Tyrell Gilbert, who made a flowery introduction that was as necessary as announcing the sun would rise in the morning. Everyone knew who the women were and what they were going to do, but they humored their host, waiting for him to finish so the women could sing.

The applause died down after Tyrell congratulated Amethyst on her twenty-five years in the music business; then the three women began to belt out a medley of Amethyst's hit records and a couple of the younger women's songs.

Courtney stepped sideways in order to see around a rather portly gentleman who was in front of her. Her movement brought her closer to the door, which was what she wanted anyway. As soon as her mother and sisters were finished, there would undoubtedly be a photograph session. That would be Courtney's cue to leave.

Sure enough, after her family was done singing, Tyrell directed them in various poses for the photographers. As Courtney continued to sidle toward the door, she tried to catch her mother's eye to let her know she was leaving. She wasn't having much luck.

"If you get any closer to the door, you'll be outside."

The low male voice sent shivers of awareness along her skin. She turned her head in his direction and saw the man her mother called Denver standing close beside her. Amusement warmed his gray eyes as he looked down at her, a slight smile shaping his firm mouth.

"Being outside is the general idea," she said coolly.

"Aren't you enjoying the party?"

She shrugged. "It's all right as parties go."

"Not a fan of country-western music?"

"I'm a fan of Amethyst Rand and Amber and Crystal."

Facing her, he leaned a shoulder against the wall, his body only inches away from hers as she forced herself to stay where she was. The way he was standing parted his tuxedo jacket, exposing its red silk lining. From his patent leather shoes to his shiny black hair, he was even more devastatingly attractive close up. As aware as she was of his height and masculine presence, she couldn't help noticing his scent, a combination of spicy pine and his own male essence.

His gaze remained on her as she looked back at the women near the piano.

"They're brown," he murmured softly. "I wondered."

His odd statement had her turning her head again toward him. "Excuse me?"

"Your eyes. I've been curious about their color."

"Are you taking some sort of survey on people's eye color?" she asked, straining to keep her voice light.

He smiled. "Just yours." Reading her expression correctly, he asked, "Why do you find that so hard to believe?"

"Probably because it's not my eyes you've been looking at all night."

His gaze slowly flowed down her throat to her breasts, covered only by a thin fabric between the splashes of white lace. Her heartbeat thudded painfully in her chest when he brought his gaze back to her face.

"You're a beautiful woman," he said as though that explained everything. He lifted his hand and touched the diamond stud earring in her ear, then trailed the back of his finger down her neck. "You're a woman of contrasts. Hard diamond earrings and skin like silk. A warm smile and wary eyes. You're at the party, yet not really a part of it. I can't help being curious."

A ripple of sensation skidded down her spine when he touched her. She looked away. "Try not to be."

"I am." His chuckle was deep and low and vibrated along her nerve endings. "You have no idea how hard I'm trying to keep my hands off you."

She jerked her head around. "Look, whatever-your-name-is, I—"

"Denver."

"Look, Denver, I—"

"Sierra."

She blinked, losing her train of thought for a moment. "What?"

"My name is Denver Sierra."

She made a dismissing gesture with her hand. "It doesn't matter what your name is. What I'm trying to—"

"It matters to me," he interrupted again. "I'd rather you used my name than 'whatever-your-name-is.'"

Courtney bit her lip as she strove to find some control over her temper. If the blasted man would let her finish one sentence, she might be able to put an end to this conversation. She frowned as she tried to remember what she had been about to say.

As though he read her mind, he said, "We were talking about my having trouble keeping my hands off you."

She turned to face him directly. Planting her hands on her hips, she lifted her chin defiantly. "You need a few classes in sensitivity training, Mr. Sierra. You shouldn't—"

"Denver," he said softly.

Through clenched teeth she muttered, "If you don't stop interrupting me, I'm going to slug you."

He grinned. "Did you know your eyes flash with gold highlights when you're angry?"

Courtney tried counting to ten, but it didn't help. It was odd how quickly she'd become angry. For the last two years she'd lived in an emotionless vacuum, but Denver Sierra had yanked her out of it with only a few remarks. She wasn't grateful.

She took a deep breath, then managed to speak calmly. "This might come as a great shock to you, but it isn't the done thing to make passes at one woman when you've brought another woman to a party. It's very difficult for either woman to believe you're going to be the faithful type."

He had crossed his arms over his chest as she spoke. Still leaning against the wall, he studied her carefully, as though assessing the strength of her anger. "Would you believe I brought Amber Childs to this party as a favor to a client?"

"No."

"It's the truth. Oh, she's a beautiful woman, and I'm enjoying her company, but I doubt if I'll be seeing her again socially."

"She'll be devastated," Courtney said dryly.

His smile deepened. "I doubt it. Amber is following her mother's request, as am I. Miss Rand wanted me to see her manager's house, and her daughter needed an escort, so here I am. You haven't told me your name."

"That's true."

"It will be easier if I have a name for the woman I'll be thinking about after I take Amber home tonight."

Courtney was bemused at her reluctance to give him her name. It wasn't an unusual request for him to make—except for his reason for making it—but she didn't want to relinquish even that part of herself to him.

Feeling silly for her ridiculous thoughts, she said, "My name is Courtney."

"Is that your first name or your last?"

"First."

Satisfaction glittered in his eyes. "And your last name?"

She sighed. "Caine."

He tried her name out. "Courtney Caine. I like it. It suits you."

"My mother will be thrilled you approve."

He tilted his head slightly as he studied her. "You're very defensive with me. Is it just me or men in general?"

"I have this thing about pushy men."

"Am I being pushy simply because I want to know your name? This is a social gathering. I'm only being social."

She saw the amusement in his eyes, and the awareness. If this was his idea of being social, she wondered what his approach would be if he was after a more intimate relationship. Because that thought created an odd sensation in the pit of her stomach, she broke their eye contact.

"If you're so intent on being social," she said, "you should be mingling with the others."

"I've already done that. I'd rather mingle with you."

Since subtlety wasn't working, she tried a more direct approach. "I'm not interested."

"Yes, you are. You don't want to admit it for some reason, but you feel something too. Your eyes give you away."

"You're right," she said in a tight voice. "I do feel something. Extreme irritation. You're assuming an awful lot on such short acquaintance."

"I've found that standing by waiting for things to happen doesn't work. I wouldn't be as successful as I am if I didn't go after what I wanted."

The implication that he wanted her was there, but she didn't follow up on it. She grasped instead the change of subject with as much desperation as a drowning man reaching for a lifeline. "So you're successful at renovating houses?"

"How did you know I'm in construction?"

"I was talking to Crystal Blair a few minutes ago. She mentioned you were going to be working on Amethyst's plantation house."

He nodded, his eyes narrowing as he studied her face. "Should I be flattered you were asking her about me?"

"I didn't ask. She told me. There's a difference."

Chuckling, he stroked a finger over her jaw. "Such a stubborn little chin. You aren't going to make this easy for me, are you?" His gaze lowered from her eyes to his finger as he drew it over her bottom lip. "It doesn't matter. I have a trace of stubbornness myself. We certainly won't be bored with each other."

"Since we won't be seeing each other after tonight, I don't see how you'll ever know for sure."

He dropped his hand when he realized they were about to have company. "You'll be seeing me again,

Courtney," he said quietly, then shifted his attention to the woman approaching them.

Amber's smile was warm as she stopped beside them. "Oh, good. You two have met. I meant to introduce you earlier, but I never got the chance."

Courtney noticed Denver didn't quite know what to make of Amber's statement. Before he got a chance to ask any questions, she turned to her sister. "Crystal was telling me about Tyrell's redecorated bathroom. Have you seen it yet?"

Amber's laughter was gay and light. "I almost got a cavity while I was putting on fresh lipstick. The pink color is just too sweet."

"He must have bought the paint on sale. Green is usually his favorite color. It's the color of money."

"Shame on you, Emmy," Amber chided. "You know Tyrell is a pussy cat, really. He's only tough when it comes to contracts."

Denver looked from Amber to Courtney. "Emmy? You said your name is Courtney."

Courtney detected a trace of anger in his eyes and voice. He thought she had lied to him. She hadn't. She had just neglected to give him her full name, which was Emerald Courtney Caine. Her mother had named all of her daughters after gems.

She gave her sister a brief silencing glance, then turned back to him. "Emmy is a nickname Amber has always called me."

The glint of anger disappeared, replaced by curiosity. "Apparently you know each other well. Are you in the music business too?"

"No."

He raised an eyebrow at her blunt answer. "That was brief and not very informative."

"Emmy doesn't like to talk about herself much," Amber said as she slipped her arm through Denver's. "I, on the other hand, love to talk about myself, so come along with me. Momma wants to show you the floor tile in Tyrell's kitchen, and I've been sent to fetch you." She leaned over and kissed Courtney's cheek. "I'm glad you came tonight."

Courtney smiled. "It's been an experience." She glanced at Denver, meeting his puzzled eyes.

Amber giggled softly. "I'll bet it has." She turned and began leading Denver away. "I know this is supposed to be a social occasion," she said to him, "but Momma didn't want to miss the chance to show you Tyrell's kitchen floor while you were here. She wants your opinion on whether the same sort of tile would be appropriate in the plantation house."

Courtney watched them for a moment, then turned to walk out of the room while Denver's back was to her. The late May night was warm, so she hadn't brought a coat. Her car keys were in the hidden slit pocket in her skirt. She was more than ready to leave the party. As soon as she got home, she would swim, then work on her thesis until she was so tired, she would go right to sleep.

And forget Denver Sierra.

When Denver returned to the living room, his gaze automatically searched the room for the mysterious woman who had captivated his attention all evening. Damn, he thought when he caught no glimpse of her. She'd left. Frustration had him gritting his teeth. For the last half hour he'd tried to find out more about Courtney Caine from Amber, then Amethyst. If he could have found Crystal, he would have tried to pump her for information too. Both Amber and Amethyst had been surprisingly evasive on the subject of Courtney Caine, which made him even more curious. Neither woman was particularly reticent about any other subject. All he knew about Courtney was her name and that she appealed to him on a strictly primitive level. He wanted her.

The first time he'd seen her, he had felt as if someone had punched him in the stomach. Each time he'd looked at her after that, the same gut-wrenching need had shot through him. There had been women in his life more classically beautiful than she, more aggressive, and some who were certainly more cooperative, but none had ever affected him as strongly as she had.

Once he'd touched her, he'd had to exert an enormous amount of control not to pull her into his arms so he could taste her. Bemused by his own reaction, he wondered if it was possible to be suffering from a midlife crisis at the tender age of thirty-six. He was certainly suffering from something, but he had no idea what.

Amber had implied Courtney was a private person. So was he. That wouldn't be a problem. He intended their relationship to be very private, personal, and intimate.

His eyes narrowed as he made a promise to himself to find her, no matter what it took.

Two

Courtney sneezed for the third time in the last ten minutes. Dust floated in the cool air and coated the tops of the books on the shelves. Each time she pulled a book out, a fine layer of dust would slide off, usually in her direction. Even though the basement storage area was cleaned regularly, it always managed to retain the same amount of dust. The lighting wasn't the best, either, and the temperature was kept low to help preserve the books. The atmosphere was stuffy, as though fresh air was rarely allowed in.

It was one of Courtney's favorite places.

After an hour in the basement the white shirt she wore under her blue denim jacket wasn't as fresh as it had been. She had pulled the collar up around her neck to try to prevent dust from trickling down her back, but she could feel a light coating on her skin nonetheless. It didn't matter. She was perfectly happy to put up with the grime for the privilege of using the private research library in Colonial Williamsburg. All the information in the books on the numerous shelves had been put on microfilm, but Courtney preferred to find what she needed out of the original material, rather than stare at a small screen in the main library upstairs.

At one end of the room were two long study tables. She piled her research material on one of them, along with her carryall filled with various supplies. She didn't bother to brush off the wooden chair before she sat down. Her jeans were already covered with dust. A little more certainly wouldn't make any difference.

From the carryall she took out a thermos of coffee, a notebook, and a pair of oversized reading glasses. After slipping on the glasses and pushing up the sleeves of her jacket, she took the top book off the stack and opened it. The bare light bulb overhead gave off enough light for her to read the small print as she ran her finger over the table of contents, searching for any reference to midwives practicing their trade in the eighteenth century.

Two pages in her spiral notebook were filled with notes, and she was on her second cup of coffee when she heard footsteps on the metal stairs. She frowned at the interruption. Few people came down to the storage area on Saturdays, which was one of the reasons she had chosen to use it that day. She could only hope whoever it was would get whatever they wanted, then go away.

Tucking her hair behind her ear to keep it from falling in her way, she bent her head back over the open book, continuing to take notes as she tried to ignore the footsteps that seemed to be coming closer and closer.

A low male chuckle had her jerking her head up. Denver Sierra was leaning against the end of a book shelf, his arms crossed over his chest. His stance was similar to the way he had propped himself against the wall in Tyrell's living room a week ago, but now he was dressed in jeans and a dark green shirt, the sleeves rolled up on his forearms. He looked relaxed and casual, but she saw a predatory gleam in his eyes that hadn't been there the other night.

"You forgot to leave a shoe behind when you left the party, Cinderella," he said.

She tossed her pen down and leaned back in the chair with a sigh of resignation. "What are you doing here?"

"I told you I'd be seeing you again. You should have believed me." He pushed away from the bookshelf and walked over to the table. Pulling out the chair across from her, he sat down and peered at the binding of one of her books. "*Birth and Death in the Eighteenth Century,*" he read aloud. "Cheery topic." He picked up another and read it to himself. "Why all the interest in the medical practices of the colonial period?"

She reached over and took the book from him. "It's for a thesis I'm writing. You didn't answer my question. Why are you here? This is a private library."

"So I've been told." He leaned back in his chair, ignoring the creaking protest of the wood. "Amethyst told me where I'd find you. She said you're the person I should talk to about some of the materials she wants used in the plantation house. Imagine my surprise when she supplied the answer to a question I've been asking for the last week. How do I find Courtney Caine?"

Courtney sensed his anger, even though his voice was even and calm. Apparently he'd been looking for her since the party and hadn't been pleased at not being able to find her. She lived in Yorktown, and she knew his construction company was in Richmond, so it wasn't surprising they hadn't run into each other. She hadn't expected him to try to see her again, though. During the past week she had disregarded the provocative things he'd said to her, figuring he'd only been passing the time during the party. She hadn't taken him seriously. Maybe she should have.

Stalling, she reached for her cup of coffee and took a sip, uncomfortably aware that he was watching every move she made.

She set the cup down and poured more coffee into it. "I only have the one cup, but you can share it if you'd like some coffee."

Sitting forward, he took the cup from her. Instead of drinking from the side closest to him, he turned the cup and drank from the same place her lips had been. It was a strangely intimate gesture that had her breath shuddering in her chest.

When she slowly raised her gaze from his mouth, she felt her heartbeat quicken at the heat radiating from his eyes. "No," she murmured as though he had asked her a question.

The lines at the corners of his eyes deepened as he smiled. "Yes. You can run all you want, Courtney, but I'll catch you eventually."

His reference to her running had her lips twisting in a rueful smile. Running was one activity she'd never been able to participate in. She knew he had meant the term figuratively, not literally, but it still brought her disability to mind.

"I haven't been trying to hide from you," she said quietly.

"Then why did you leave the party without talking to me again?"

Amused at the arrogance of his question, she smiled faintly. "Evidently I missed something during our conversation the other night. We barely exchanged names. I'm sure I would have remembered if we'd made any long-term commitment. Why don't you just tell me what my mother wants me to—" She stopped when she saw shock widen his eyes. "What's the matter?"

He got to his feet and spread his hands palm down on the table as he leaned toward her. "Amethyst Rand is your mother?"

Only when he asked the question did she realize he hadn't known. Even though she'd rarely appeared in public with her family in the last two years, it was common knowledge among Amethyst's associates who she was.

"Obviously you're finding that hard to believe, but yes, Amethyst Rand is my mother."

Denver looked at her long and hard before walking around to her side of the table. Her stubborn little chin was raised in a defensive gesture, as it had been the night he'd met her. Shoving her notebook and a book out of the way, he half sat on the edge of the table. "I'll be damned," he muttered under his breath.

"Probably," she said with as much bravado as she could muster. She sat as far back as she could in her chair, but he was still too close, too overwhelming. "Now that we've got that out of the way, what information did my mother want me to look up for you?"

"We'll get to that eventually. Right now I want to know why you and your family are so secretive about your relationship."

Short of walking away from him, which, considering the stairs, would take a while, there wasn't much she could do except answer him. "They choose to be public figures. I don't. It's the last thing I want. You saw the reporters the other night at Tyrell's, taking pictures, asking questions. If they had known I was Amethyst's daughter, they would want to know why I wasn't also singing with the Jewels of the South. They would want to take my picture with my mother and sisters. My family protects me by keeping my identity a secret from the press."

"I don't know why they think you need protecting. You managed just fine on your own the other night. We talked for about ten minutes, and all I learned about you was your name." He paused and looked at her with a puzzled expression. "Why do your mother and sisters all have names of jewels and you don't?"

Her smile was a little off center. "I do. My full name is Emerald Courtney Caine."

Amusement gleamed in his eyes. "Which explains why Amber calls you Emmy."

"Afraid so."

"Since you've given away some of your deepest,

darkest secrets, how about telling me why you want to keep your identity a secret."

She gave him part of the reason for her reticence. "I doubt if my students would take me seriously if they saw their history teacher's photograph in one of those tabloids at the checkout counter in the local grocery store. I don't need publicity like that."

His gaze never left her face, his expression searching and curious. "You're a history teacher?"

She tilted her head up. "Yes, I am. Do you have a problem with that?"

"No," he drawled, smiling at the way she led with her chin. "I don't have a problem with that."

Without warning he reached down and grabbed both ends of her turned-up collar, drawing her up out of the chair. When she stumbled, he slid his hands to her arms to steady her. He heard something hard strike the leg of the chair, but by then he had brought her between his spread thighs, her mouth only inches from his.

"I don't have any problems with what you do," he said huskily. "The only thing I'm having a problem with is how you affect me. I haven't had a decent night's sleep since I saw you last Saturday night. Wondering how you taste has kept me awake." His hands dropped to her waist and drew her closer. "It's time I found out."

When his mouth touched hers, Courtney felt a jolt of pleasure. Instinctively she parted her lips to open herself for more. She sighed into the warmth of his mouth as he deepened the kiss, taking her further into an unfamiliar world of sensuality. His thighs tightened around her hips as his hands slid under her jacket, bringing her even closer.

It had been so long since she'd felt the warmth and strength of a man's body. She shouldn't be enjoying this, she told herself. After what Philip had done to her, she should be repulsed by a man's touch, but she wasn't. There was no fear that Denver would hurt her, only exquisite pleasure.

She heard him suck in his breath as his hand stroked the length of her back without running into any interference. She could tell the moment he discovered she wasn't wearing anything under her shirt.

Denver raised his head and looked down at her, his breath coming hard in an effort to restrain himself. When she pressed her hands against his chest in resistance, he relinquished his hold on her and let her step back. It was either that or pull her down onto the table. If he'd ever wanted a woman as badly as he wanted Courtney Caine, he couldn't remember it. She had him tied in knots without even trying to attract him. He didn't want to think about how he would react if she did try. Since he'd met her a week ago, he'd been constantly in a state of semiarousal, needing only the thought of the way the white lace had hugged her breasts to make him so hard, he ached.

He shouldn't have kissed her, he thought wildly, clamping down on the need to pull her back into his arms. Her response when he kissed her was everything he could possibly want, but it made it more difficult for him to keep from taking her completely.

"Have lunch with me," he murmured. "In a

crowded restaurant where I won't be able to kiss you again."

She shook her head. "No."

He watched as she sank down into the chair, her movements oddly uncoordinated, which pleased him in a purely masculine way. He wasn't the only one who was reeling from the effects of that kiss.

Straightening, he stepped around the table, putting it between them. His gaze focused on her mouth, still moist from his, and he clenched his hands into fists to keep from reaching for her again. An unreasonable anger blended with the desire tightening his body. It didn't make any sense, but he resented her for making him feel this way, as though his insides were caught in a giant vise that wouldn't be released until he buried himself deep inside her.

Since he was still able to think fairly rationally, he knew they had a ways to go before she would accept him as a lover. Somehow he would find the patience to wait until her needs were as strong as his.

Reaching into his back pocket, he withdrew a folded piece of paper and held it out to her.

She didn't take it. "What is that?" she asked, frowning.

"A list of questions I have on building materials I'll need for your mother's plantation house. Some of the supplies I can get from my regular sources, but there are some we'd like to make ourselves. When I told Amethyst it would take me some time to research the type of materials we need, she suggested I see you."

For a moment Courtney simply stared at him.

From what he'd said earlier, he had asked Amethyst and her sisters about her without any luck. Now her mother had changed her mind and told him where to find her. Evidently Amethyst trusted Denver, or she wouldn't have sent him to her. It might have taken him longer, but he could have found out what he wanted to know in other ways.

She took the paper from him and unfolded it. At the top was the letterhead of Sierra Construction, Custom Builders, giving an address in Richmond, several phone numbers, and the names Denver Sierra and Phoenix Sierra.

"Phoenix?" she asked.

"My brother."

"Denver and Phoenix," she murmured.

"I know." The amusement was back in his voice. "It sounds like destinations on a road map. My mother was born in Colorado and raised in Arizona. She was part Navaho Indian. My father said he settled for Denver and Phoenix when the only other choices my mother gave him were Wild Wolf and Tame Wolf."

Now she knew why he resembled the Indian in the painting. "Let me guess," she said, smiling. "You were to be Wild Wolf."

Denver looked for any change in her eyes when she learned he was part Indian. He didn't find any, other than amusement over his name. "How'd you guess?" he asked.

"A stab in the dark. Are you the oldest?"

"By two years. Are you going to read the list, or do you want to know how much I weighed when I was born?"

The glare she sent him could have stripped paint

off a wall. "Your mother should have named you Grumpy Wolf."

His laughter startled her, then made her smile. Something deep inside her responded to him on a primitive level whether he was laughing or scowling. All he had to do was look at her, and she became aware of him as a man. To force her mind away from her response to him, she looked at the paper in her hand.

His handwriting was neat and easy to read, and she skimmed down the list of items. Even though there weren't many topics, it would take a bit of research to find the details he wanted. Just under the heading of bricks alone were at least five questions, such as temperature of firing; formula for the clay, sand, and water mixture; consistency; size of molds.

She looked up at him. "Why do you want to know how bricks were made in the eighteenth century? There are several brick makers in the area who could fill any order you give them."

"Phoenix wants to try his hand at making them the way they were made in the eighteenth century. The amount needed for your mother's plantation alone is staggering. She wants all the outbuildings that are on the original set of plans you found for her rebuilt. We also have several other jobs pending where we could use the colonial bricks."

"If I can keep this list for a couple of days, I'll find the information you need."

Denver's original intention had been to do exactly that, but that was before he'd seen her again. Now he didn't want to leave her. At least not yet. "Point me in the right direction, tell me what you want, and I'll start collecting some of the literature you'll need."

"You don't have to do that," she said quickly. "I work better alone."

He ignored her protest. She was going to have to get used to having him around. "I'll start on the bricks, since Phoenix wants to get going as soon as possible with building a kiln. You can work on whatever you came here to do while I dig around to find the stuff he needs to know. Where do you suggest I start looking?"

Courtney sighed. She had the sinking feeling that trying to divert Denver Sierra from the path he was intent on taking would be like trying to bail the James River dry with a spoon. She tore a sheet of paper from her spiral notebook and handed it to him, along with a pen she took out of her carryall.

"Write," she ordered.

He sat down. "Yes, ma'am," he murmured as he obediently picked up the pen in his left hand.

Looking up at the ceiling, as if the information could be found there, she began to dictate. "First, Phoenix could check with the department of Colonial Building Trades here in Colonial Williamsburg. They have a kiln for making bricks that he could examine. Next, go to the card file and look up all references to bricks, brick makers, ceramics, ancient trades, and crafts—"

She stopped when he said gruffly, "Not so fast."

Smiling, she continued listing other references, slower this time. After giving him enough to keep him busy for at least an hour, she pulled her own research material back in front of her while he walked over to the card file at the opposite end of the room.

She had been humoring him when she'd given in to his demand to help. Denver Sierra didn't impress her as the type of man who could sit still for hours leafing through books. He seemed too restless, too active for the time-consuming business of research.

She was right. After forty-five minutes of walking up and down the aisles and plunking books down on the other end of her table, he suggested they break for lunch.

Concentrating on the paragraph she was reading, she said, "You go ahead if you want. I still have a lot to get through."

"Aren't you going to take a break?"

"Maybe later."

"I don't see how you can sit there for hours at a time reading. My eyes are crossing."

"I'm made of stern stuff," she drawled. "I do have a lot to do, Denver. I brought a sandwich to eat while I work. I'd share it with you, except I think you have a case of cabin fever. You go ahead. I'm fine here."

He didn't like it, but he accepted her refusal as graciously as he could. "I'll be back in an hour."

Courtney sat back in her chair and watched him leave, taking the stairs two at a time with as much ease as he did everything else. If she were making a list of all the ways they didn't match, she would have to add the fact that he was athletic, very physical. It was apparent in the way he moved like a coiled spring, yet with a lithe grace that made it a pleasure simply to watch him stride across a room.

Levering her legs under her, she stood up and walked the length of the table, looking down as she took one step after the other. Her gait was slow and measured, nothing like Denver's swift, smooth stride. Walking with her would require him to adjust his steps to her pace. There would be places she couldn't go with him, things she couldn't do with him, and he would begin to resent the restrictions she had known all her life. Like Philip had. She had nothing to offer Denver but problems he didn't need.

Somehow she would have to discourage him when he pushed to see her again. And she knew he was going to push.

After walking around the table several times, she sat down again and tried to concentrate on her work. Now that she was alone, though, she had the chance to think about why her mother had sent Denver after her. She had a feeling she already knew why. Amethyst apparently liked Denver and trusted him with more than the renovations on her plantation. She trusted him with her daughter. Considering how protective Amethyst had been toward Courtney the last two years, it was quite a concession for the older woman to make.

Maybe her mother trusted Denver, but Courtney didn't trust the way he made her feel just by walking into the room.

Sighing, she shoved her glasses onto her nose and picked up her pen. Working on her thesis was more constructive than trying to second-guess her mother's motives. Or Denver's. Or her own.

One of the things that appealed to her about history was that it was permanent. Nothing could change what had already happened. The past could be analyzed, memorized, and examined, but it couldn't be altered. Lessons could be learned from the events and actions of people down through the ages. Seeing the mistakes others had made in the past served as an example, a lesson why errors in judgment shouldn't be repeated.

Her own history had an error in judgment she wasn't going to make again, Courtney thought. She'd better keep reminding herself about Philip and what he'd said the last time she'd seen him.

When she heard the sound of western boots on the metal steps, she looked up and saw Denver ducking his head so he didn't hit the overhang as he came down the stairs. He was so tall, so overwhelmingly attractive, so aggressively male. Her heart thudded uncomfortably as he came closer.

Like an incantation, she kept saying over and over in her mind, *Remember Philip. Remember Philip.*

A white paper bag was tucked in the crook of his arm. He set it down when he reached the table and began unloading the contents.

"I took a chance on you liking Mexican food," he said.

She unwrapped the paper from one of the bundles he'd set in front of her, and an enticing aroma rose from the taco inside. The scent alone had her mouth watering. She picked up a bit of shredded cheese from the paper and watched as he continued to unload the bag. There was a sizable mound of paper-wrapped bundles when he finished.

"Good Lord, Denver. How many tacos did you buy?"

He shrugged and sat down in the chair across from her. "A dozen. Do you want medium or hot?

"Medium or hot what?"

"Sauce to put on your taco."

"Medium."

He reached in the bag again and took out several soft plastic packets, handing her one. "Dig in," he said, and unwrapped a taco for himself.

Pushing aside her stack of books, she did just that. To her astonishment she ate three before she was finished. She sat back in her chair, wondering if she was ever going to be able to move again. Denver was still eating.

"Do you mind if I ask you a question?"

He shook his head. "What do you want to know?"

"You wear western boots, you like Mexican food, you were born in Arizona, yet you live in Virginia. Why?"

He crumbled up the wrapper of his fifth taco. "My parents were divorced when I was ten and Phoenix eight. We spent the summers with my mother on the reservation in Arizona, and the rest of the year with my father, who has a large horse-breeding farm about a hundred miles from here. Because he had the financial means to support us better than my mother, he got custody. That's how Phoenix and I ended up in Virginia."

"From horses to houses is quite a jump."

"My father used to travel to different races and horse auctions all over the world, and we were left alone most of the time. When we weren't riding horses, we would hang around the guys who were doing the various renovations my father was always making around the farm. We became friends with one of the carpenters, Charlie Plunkett, who taught us how to read blueprints, handle various tools, and try our hands at some of the work."

"How did you end up in Richmond?"

"When Charlie was ready to start his own business, he decided to specialize in custom work and renovating old buildings. By then my mother had died, so there was no reason for us to go back to Arizona. She had no family except us. There'd been a resurgence of interest in restoring some of the beautiful old buildings in and around Richmond, so Charlie had more work than he could handle. We worked for him during the summer while we were attending the College of William and Mary, and when he was ready to retire, we ended up buying him out."

"You and your brother must be very close if you can work together."

His gaze settled on her mouth, then rose to meet her dark eyes. "We don't do everything together." He leaned his arms on the table. "Why don't you sing with the rest of your family? From what I saw the other night at Tyrell Gilbert's party, you all seem to get along all right."

"We get along just fine," she said evasively. She wasn't ready to tell him about her disability. Since she didn't plan on seeing him again, it shouldn't matter what his reaction would be. But it did. She didn't want to see the look in his eyes that she'd seen in Philip's. "I'm just not cut out for all that goes with being a professional singer."

He didn't make any comment for a minute. He just watched her. "Did you always want to be a teacher?" he finally asked.

"No."

He waited for her to elaborate. When he realized she wasn't going to say anything more, he asked, "What did you want instead?"

Her mouth twisted in a mocking smile. "To be a ballet dancer." He wouldn't understand the irony of her statement, and she wasn't going to explain. Tearing her gaze from his, she picked up her pen. "I need to get back to work."

Denver couldn't pin down what was wrong with her answer, and she was making it clear that was all she was going to say on the subject. Maybe it wasn't so much what she'd said as the way she'd said it, he decided.

He managed to force his attention away from her, burying it in facts and figures for an hour until his eyes glazed over. Running his fingers impatiently through his hair, he tipped his chair back and broke the silence.

"What time will you be through here?"

Courtney looked up. She'd been aware of his growing restlessness. First he'd just tapped his pen on the table, then he'd continually shifted in his chair.

"The library closes at five on Saturdays," she answered.

He looked shocked. "You're going to stay here all day?"

"Probably," she said with amusement. "I have a lot of research to do."

"The books aren't going anywhere. How about if we call it quits and go do something?"

She smiled. "Can't take it, huh?"

"I've never been very good at just sitting around.

I know I said I'd help, but this is driving me up the wall. Come with me."

Remember Philip, she told herself. "Sorry. I can't."

To her surprise he didn't try to change her mind. "You do what you have to do here," he said instead, "and I'll pick you up later tonight. We can go out to dinner, maybe go for a drive. Whatever you want to do. You'll have to tell me where you live."

"No."

The front legs of his chair hit the floor with some force. "Why not?"

"I have other plans."

"Like what?"

"They're my plans. I don't have to tell you what they are." She bent her head over her book and began writing in her notebook again.

He took the pen out of her hand. "Dammit, Courtney. Look at me."

Slowly raising her head, she did as he asked. Her expression was politely blank.

"Why won't you go out with me?" he asked.

"I told you. I have other plans."

His eyes narrowed as he studied her. "Then how about tomorrow?"

She shook her head. "I have other plans."

"So you've said. Repeatedly. Is there someone else?"

He'd given her an out, and Courtney could have taken it, but she didn't. "If you mean, am I involved with any other man, the answer is no. I don't plan on getting involved with anyone, including you. Let's leave it at that. I'll see that you get the information you want in a couple of days. Other than that we don't have any reason to see each other again."

He stood up, rounded the table, and drew her out of her chair almost before she was aware he'd moved. His grip on her upper arms was hard but not hurtful as he held her in front of him, his face only inches from hers.

"There are other reasons why you'll be seeing me again, Courtney." He lowered his head. "This is one of them."

Expecting anger, Courtney was unprepared for the explosion of desire that engulfed her the moment his mouth covered hers. The feel of his lips on hers was deliciously sensual, warming her blood and heating her skin. His hands skimmed over her back as he deepened the kiss, and she couldn't stop the sound of need from escaping her throat.

For a moment she gave in to the urges of her body, arching into his hardness, relishing his quick intake of breath. His hands clamped over her hips to hold her to his lower body, slowly grinding her against him until they were both breathing heavily.

Denver broke away from her mouth and buried his lips against her throat. He relished the aching pleasure for a few seconds more, then released her, moving her away from him. As badly as he wanted to feel her moist body closing around him, he didn't want their first time to be on a dusty book-covered table.

Looking down at her, he was gratified to see the glazed desire in her dark eyes. He was going to make sure she looked at him like that often.

"Now tell me you don't want to see me again."

Courtney's lips parted, but nothing came out. Her eyes were wide with the shock of her own reaction, her vulnerability and the attraction she didn't want to feel. All she could manage was a slight shake of her head.

An unexpected tenderness welled up in Denver like a rushing tide, and he smiled. "Never mind. I already have my answer. You do what you have to do, Courtney, and I'll do what I have to do."

She could only stare at him until he lowered his head once more and kissed her briefly. Then he left her. Stunned, she watched him stride away, again taking the stairs two at a time.

She sank down into her chair and took a deep steadying breath, but it didn't help. Denver Sierra was like a box of fireworks, exploding with a burst of color and heat, and leaving behind a fury of unforgettable sensations.

Three

It took Courtney five days to gather all the information Denver had requested, and another three days to gather the nerve to call him. During her lunch hour she used the phone in the teacher's lounge at school, hoping to catch him in his office.

The woman who answered the phone had a sultry southern drawl, which made Sierra Construction sound like something out of *Gone with the Wind.*

"I'd like to speak to Denver Sierra if he isn't busy. This is Courtney Caine."

There was a brief pause before the woman said, "Now ain't that a coincidence. He was just talking about you, and here you are callin'."

Since Courtney didn't know what to think about the woman's remark, she asked, "Is he there?"

"Honey, he's been hopping around here like a flea in a dog kennel all morning. Let me see if I can find 'em for you."

Courtney held the phone out and stared blankly at the receiver, baffled by the woman. When a male voice came over the line, saying her name, she brought the receiver back to her ear. "Denver?"

"Sorry, Courtney. This is Phoenix, Denver's brother. Belle's out looking for him. He was just in the office a minute ago, so he can't be too far away. I didn't want you hanging on the line thinking she forgot about you. We've been considering getting one of those contraptions that play music while people are on hold, but for now you're stuck with me. I could hum something if you like."

She choked back a laugh. "I'll pass, thanks." Getting back to the purpose of her call, she said, "You could give Denver a message if you would. He asked me to do some research for him regarding the Mallory plantation. Tell him I'll put it in—"

"Did you find out how bricks were made?"

Apparently interrupting people was a family trait, she thought with some amusement. "Yes, I have all of that information, including the plans for a brickworks that existed in 1780. If you'll tell Denver I'm putting everything in the mail, I'd appreciate it."

"I don't think that's a very good idea, Courtney. He'll want to see you. Why don't you drop them off here? That way I can meet you. I'd like to see the woman who's been driving my brother crazy." She overheard some muted sounds in the background, then Phoenix muttered, "Here comes Chief Thundercloud now. It's been nice talking with you, Courtney. I—"

This time Phoenix was the one cut off mid-sentence. A few seconds later Denver's familiar voice came on the line. "Courtney?"

It was odd how her heartbeat accelerated just at the sound of his voice. "Yes."

She could hear Phoenix and a woman speaking, but she couldn't make out what they were saying since they were both talking at once. She had to smile when Denver muttered a curse under his breath.

"Phoenix and Belle want you to come here," he said, "but I'm not exposing you to them just yet."

She grasped for familiar ground. "I have the information you wanted about the renovations you're doing for Momma. I'll put them in the mail today. You should get them tomorrow or the next day."

Along with the voices in the background Courtney heard the jangle of another telephone adding to the chaos. Sounding like a man stretched to the limits of his patience, Denver said, "Forget mailing it. I'll be by to get them later today."

His comment didn't go over well with his brother or the woman she assumed was his secretary. The volume of their protests rose, and she heard Denver yell, "Answer the damn phone, Belle." A second later he growled, "Dammit, Phoenix. You glued my coffee cup to the desk again."

His voice became stronger as he evidently brought the phone back to his mouth. "I have to go, Courtney. This place is more of a madhouse than usual. I'll see you later."

She opened her mouth to protest, then closed it again when she heard the dial tone in her ear. Frowning, she replaced the receiver. She was tempted to call again to tell him she was mailing the papers to him no matter what he said, but the bell announcing the start of afternoon classes stopped her. Maybe it was just as well she didn't have a chance to phone him back, she decided as she picked up the manila envelope containing the information. Denver had hung up on her once. She wasn't going to give him another chance. If Belle or Phoenix answered, it was doubtful they would simply take a message, considering their odd reactions to her.

All afternoon she half expected to see Denver stroll into her classroom. She wouldn't put it past him to appear out of the blue, whether it was an appropriate time or not.

When the final bell rang, she breathed a sigh of relief. It had been one of those days when the students were unusually restless, no matter what she did to try to gain their attention. Only three days were left in the school year, and thoughts of summer vacation were crowding out any desire to review the subjects that would be on the final test they would take the next day. The dates and details of various Civil War battles couldn't compete with the temptations of the upcoming lazy days of summer.

After she'd taken her purse out of the bottom desk drawer, Courtney locked the desk. The final-exam papers were in the principal's safe, along with other class tests. After several incidents of enterprising students "borrowing" copies of tests found in teachers' desk drawers, the principal had insisted all examination papers be left in his office. In the morning she would sign for the stack of history exams, then hand them out to the groaning students.

As she cleared off her desk, she noticed the manila envelope addressed to Denver. For a moment she simply stared at it. It was ready for mailing, except for the postage. She had planned to drop it off at the post office on her way home, but it was too late in the day. She tried to remember if she had enough stamps at home to mail the bulky envelope, but doubted it. As far as she knew, Denver didn't have her home address, but that didn't mean he couldn't get it. All he had to do was call her mother. She debated phoning Amethyst first to ask her not to give her address to Denver, but her mother would want to know why she didn't want to see him, which would lead to a discussion Courtney would rather avoid. Resigning herself to seeing Denver again, she stuffed the envelope into her carryall.

When she reached her car, she didn't notice anything unusual until she'd placed her purse on the front fender to dig out her keys. A white piece of paper had been folded and tucked under the windshield wiper on the driver's side. She leaned over to remove it, then unfolded it. On the sheet of ruled school paper, she read: "Make the test ezy or I'll make yore life hard."

Aside from the misspelled words, Courtney understood the content of the message. She glanced around, but couldn't see anyone watching her. There were a couple of other teachers heading for their cars, a janitor emptying some trash in the dumpster, but no one was looking in her direction.

She refolded the warning and stuck it into her purse.

The drive home took twice as long as usual due to an accident that had traffic at a standstill. The sun was hot and searing through the windshield as she edged along the road, caught in the string of cars. Her air conditioner kept her from sweltering, but it did nothing to ease her impatience.

Finally she was able to turn off onto the quiet street where she lived in a sprawling modern-style house, with numerous skylights and attractive cedar clapboards. Her father had bought the single-story dwelling for her when she'd graduated from college. She would have preferred to live more simply, but she hadn't the heart to hurt her father when he'd presented her with the house. Randall Caine had bought it out of love for the daughter he had rarely seen while she was growing up, and out of a sense of guilt for the same reason.

As it turned out, she'd needed the room, since her mother had insisted Courtney have their housekeeper live with her. Amethyst rarely interfered with Courtney's life, but when she did, there was little Courtney could do to dissuade her. Even though she wanted to be independent, Courtney had been forced to make the one concession of having Bronwyn MacNider live with her. It wasn't that big a hardship. Brownie, as they all called her, kept the house in order, cooked simple meals, and was good company. The housekeeper had never treated Courtney any differently from the other two girls the whole time they were growing up, never made Courtney feel she was getting preferential treatment because of her disability.

Courtney turned into her driveway and pushed the remote-control device to open the garage door, then parked her four-year-old sedan inside. Carrying her bag in one hand with her purse slung over her shoulder, she pushed open the door leading from the garage into the utility room off the kitchen.

Brownie was taking clothes out of the dryer and asked the question she always asked when Courtney came home. "How was your day?"

"Fine, aside from the fact the students are counting the hours before summer vacation. The last thing they want to do is think about the final exam tomorrow."

Tucking back a stray lock of hair that had fallen from the tightly wound bun at the base of her neck, the older woman smiled. "The exuberance of youth is a wondrous thing."

"So is paying attention in class, but I can't really blame them. I'm looking forward to vacation too."

Brownie plopped the sheet she'd just folded on top of the dryer and stuck her hands on her ample hips. "I don't know why. You'll be burying your nose in books all summer, working on your thesis. Why you want to spend all your time studying is beyond me. You already have several college degrees. Now you want another one." Reaching for another sheet from the dryer, she mumbled, "What you need is a man and a houseful of children. That's what you need, not another diploma."

"That's what you've been telling all of us since we grew out of our beginner bras, Brownie."

"Well, it hasn't done much good. None of you seem to be ready to settle down."

Too tired to go through the usual arguments, Courtney started walking out of the utility room. "I'll be in the pool, Brownie." Stopping in the doorway, she added, "I hope you haven't gone to too much trouble for dinner. I'm not very hungry."

The housekeeper's sharp gaze took in the weary slump of Courtney's shoulders, and concern made her voice harsher than she intended. "You work entirely too much, Courtney, and you don't eat enough to keep a bird alive."

"Actually, a bird eats a great deal, contrary to what people think."

"Schoolteachers think they know everything." Gesturing with her hand, Brownie shooed Courtney away. "Go do your exercises. I'll fix a salad for you when you're through."

"Thanks, Brownie."

Courtney wasn't so tired she wasn't aware of the careful way the housekeeper was holding her head, as though there were a distinct possibility it might fall off.

"Your headache's back, isn't it?"

Turning away, Brownie mumbled, "A little."

"Why don't you go lie down and rest for a while? Forget the salad. I'll fix myself something later."

"Don't be silly. I'm fine."

Courtney didn't believe her, but she knew it wouldn't do any good to try to convince Brownie to take it easy. She'd tried before to talk Brownie into going to a doctor, but without success. She'd have to think of something else.

As she passed through the living room, she glanced out the sliding glass door that led to the swimming pool. Beau was padding back and forth across the covered patio. The Siberian husky had his own sense of time and somehow always knew when she was due to arrive home. The dog had been a gift from Amber and Crystal when she'd moved into the house. Not only was he an intimidating watchdog, but he had quickly learned to fetch things for her, once he'd gotten past the chew-everything-in-sight puppy stage.

After she'd stripped off her clothes and put on her blue-and-green metallic print bikini, Courtney slipped into an oversized gauze shirt. Towels, lotion, and whatever else was needed for anyone using the pool were kept in a small alcove off the patio, so she didn't need to take anything with her.

Beau greeted her with his usual enthusiasm, his light blue eyes glittering with joy at seeing her. He had never once jumped up on her since she'd had him. It was as though he knew he would unbalance her. He saved that particular antic for Brownie, who tolerated the animal for Courtney's sake.

Beau remained beside her as she walked slowly to the pool. He sat down on his haunches beside the chaise longue as she removed the fasteners to her brace, his pink tongue trailing out of his mouth as he panted from the heat of the early summer evening.

Courtney laid the brace beside her on the chaise, then covered it with her shirt. Beau stood up when she did, moving to her side so she could use him as a support while she limped to the edge of the pool. After patting his head as a reward for his assistance, Courtney put her weight on her good leg, took a deep breath, and dived into the deep end.

The water sluiced over her heated skin like cool satin. Breaking the surface, she began the laps she did every day.

While she was on her fifth lap, she saw Brownie standing near the shallow end. Rubbing her hand over her eyes to wipe off the water, Courtney looked up at the housekeeper, surprised to see a frown on the older woman's usually placid face.

"What is it, Brownie?"

"There's a man here to see you. He said you were expecting him. Since you hadn't mentioned anyone would be coming over tonight, I left him in the living room until I talked to you."

Courtney didn't need to ask if the man had given her his name. There was only one person it could be. Denver Sierra.

"There's a manila envelope in the carryall I brought home with me. Give it to him. It's what he wants."

Suddenly the hair on the back of Beau's neck bristled, and a low growl rumbled deep in his throat.

"It's not all I want," a man said from behind Brownie.

Approaching the dog slowly, Denver extended his hand toward the husky, who had moved between him and Courtney. Denver bent his knees, hunkering down so he was less threatening, and putting himself in a dangerous position if the dog decided to charge him.

"Here," he murmured in a soft, soothing voice. "Get used to my scent, fella. I'm not going to hurt your mistress. You'll have to take my word for it, just like she does."

After a thorough scent survey of the offered hand, the dog relaxed his vigil, though he still remained between Denver and Courtney. So did Brownie.

Courtney resigned herself to having to deal with Denver now that he was there. "It's all right, Brownie. Mr. Sierra is the contractor Momma hired to do the renovations on the Mallory plantation. Denver, this is Bronwyn MacNider."

Standing up, Denver held out his hand. "It's a pleasure to meet you."

Brownie was still frowning, but she carried out the social amenities by shaking his hand.

"Brownie," Courtney said, "would you mind getting the envelope out of my room please? It's information Mr. Sierra needs."

Brownie looked long and hard at Denver, then shifted her gaze to Courtney. "I'll leave the door open in case you need to call me."

Hiding her smile, Courtney answered, "I'll be all right, Brownie."

With another sharp look in Denver's direction Brownie returned to the house, making a point of leaving the sliding door open as she had said she would.

Having made a friend of the dog, Denver placed his hand on the husky's head as he let his gaze flow over the woman in the pool. She was standing in water that came up to her ribs. The lower part of her body was distorted by the water, but he was able to see the bare flesh between the shimmering piece of cloth that covered her breasts and the triangular scrap of material below it.

His fingers clenched in the dog's fur as his body tightened painfully. He wanted to run his hands over her slick skin, to feel the textures and shapes of her body. He was actually jealous of the water for having the privilege of caressing her bare flesh.

Needing to concentrate on something other than the thought of stripping off his clothes and jumping into the pool with her, he said, "I guess I don't have to worry about you. You have quite a security team."

She smiled. "Brownie has been a friend of the family for as long as I can remember."

"Does she live here with you?"

"Yes. She keeps the house from turning into a dust heap and cooks most of our meals."

Courtney watched as he glanced around, taking in the landscaped grounds beyond the pool, then the house itself. As an experienced contractor he would be able to put a fairly accurate price tag on the house and property. He wouldn't be the first person to wonder how she could afford such an expensive house on a teacher's salary. Since he knew of her relationship with Amethyst, though, he probably assumed her mother had provided the house for her.

"It's my father's house," she said, not sure why she felt compelled to explain.

"I didn't ask."

"Yes, you did. Just not aloud. There aren't many schoolteachers who have a large place like this with a pool and a housekeeper. It would be strange if you didn't wonder how I could afford it."

"There aren't many schoolteachers whose mother is a music star."

"That's true, but my father bought the house, not my mother."

He tilted his head to one side, assessing her carefully. "It's hard to imagine you as the daughter of Randall Caine. From what I've read about him, he eats nails for breakfast and thinks no more of gobbling up businesses than he does snapping his fingers."

"You shouldn't believe everything you read in the newspapers. According to one enterprising news-magazine, my mother has been married six times. She's been married three. Speaking of my mother, would I be correct in assuming you got my address from her?"

"You would be correct. She even gave me directions."

Courtney's look of irritation wasn't caused only by her mother, who was suddenly being so free with her whereabouts. She had a problem. She couldn't stay in the pool forever. The sun had disappeared under some threatening clouds, cooling the air drastically. To remain in the pool much longer would look odd, but there had to be a better way to introduce him to her disability.

She decided to stall until she could figure out how to broach the subject. "You didn't have to come here tonight. I told you I would send the material to you."

He stroked the dog's coarse fur, his gaze never leaving her. "I didn't come because I thought I had to. I wanted to see you again."

"Denver . . . ," she began hesitantly. "I don't

think it would be a good idea if we became person-
ally involved."

It was already too late for that warning, Denver
thought distractedly. Two steps brought him to
the edge of the pool, where he bent down to bring
himself closer to her level. "Why not?"

She struggled to come up with a reason that
would sound plausible. "We don't have much in
common."

He grinned and held out his hand toward her.
"Why don't you come out of there, and I'll show you
how much we have in common."

Thunder rumbled across the darkening sky, and
she glanced up. "It looks like it's going to rain. Why
don't you go into the house? I'll join you in a
minute."

He still held his hand out to her. "Didn't your
mother ever tell you it's not a good idea to remain
in a pool during a storm?"

Raindrops began to make little circles on the
surface of the water around her. A loud clap of
thunder vibrated in the air. Resigned, she moved
to the edge of the pool. Ignoring the offer of his
hand, she pulled herself out of the water and sat
on the edge. "Beau," she said, looking at the dog,
"fetch."

The husky brought her shirt first, dropping it
onto the concrete beside her, then returned to
the chaise for the brace. She could feel Denver's
gaze on her as she fitted to her foot the high-top
shoe attached to the metal brace, then fastened
the straps around her leg.

The rain fell more heavily as the seconds passed,
but Denver made no move to duck into the house.

He stood several feet away, not offering to help her, just steadily watching as she placed her hand on the dog's back and levered herself up to a standing position.

Courtney half expected him to pick her up and carry her into the house, but he didn't. He simply stood in the rain, getting thoroughly drenched, his gaze never leaving her. She wished she knew what he was thinking. His face looked as if it had been carved out of stone.

With the dog at her side she walked toward the house. Denver fell into step beside her, not attempting to rush her or assist her in any way. When she reached the alcove under the covered patio, she opened a door and removed a couple of folded towels. After handing one to him she rubbed her arms, her face, and her hair. She left her wet shirt in the alcove and took out a long robe made of a heavy toweling fabric. She concentrated on rolling up the sleeves several turns, wishing Denver would say something, anything to break the tension arcing between them.

She rubbed Beau's heavy coat with another towel to remove as much of the rain as she could. When she left the alcove to walk to the sliding door, she didn't need to tell Beau to stay. The large dog simply sat down by the door, watching Denver follow her into the house.

Courtney hitched the belt of her robe tighter as she slowly walked to the front entry hall, more conscious of her limp than ever before in her life. Stopping near the door, she picked up the manila envelope Brownie had placed on the table there. She was as prepared as she would ever be to face the man behind her. Her breath caught in her throat when she looked up and saw the raw fury blazing in his eyes.

"Here," she said quietly, extending the envelope toward him. "This is what you came for."

He took the envelope from her and tossed it back onto the table. "I'm not leaving until we talk."

"Denver, I'm wet. So are you. I—"

"I've been wet before. It's not a terminal condition. Go change into dry clothes."

"What about you?"

"Unless you have clothes in my size, I'll stay as I am." He ran his fingers through his damp hair in a gesture of impatience. "Go change, Courtney. I'm not leaving."

She did as he ordered. In her room she stripped off her wet suit and put on fresh underwear, then slipped into a pair of tan slacks and a white cotton sweater. Moving to the bathroom off her room, she towel-dried her hair, then ran a comb through it. Slicking the still-damp hair back, she gathered it at the nape of her neck with a clasp.

When she came out of her room, Denver was leaning against the opposite wall, waiting for her. He had removed his soaked shirt, and the sight of his bare chest sent a flashfire of heat through her. His jeans were low on his hips, exposing a wide expanse of tanned skin covered lightly with dark curling hair.

"Your friend took my shirt," he said. "She's going to dry it for me. I talked her out of taking my jeans."

Pushing away from the wall, he took her arm to turn her toward the living room. As he had before, he paced his step to accommodate hers until they reached the living room. Releasing her arm, he took several steps away, then turned to pin her with his furious gaze.

Four

"Now I know why your mother wants an elevator installed in the plantation house," he said, his voice quiet but intense. "I thought it was an odd request when she wanted everything else authentically eighteenth century." For a long moment he continued to look at her; then he murmured, "I don't believe it."

It wasn't what she'd thought he would say. Nor did she see the look of pity she'd expected. Anger, perhaps, and maybe disbelief, but she couldn't see any sign of sympathy in his eyes as he continued to look at her.

"You're going to have to believe it," she said. "This brace isn't a fashion accessory."

"That's not what I meant. I find it hard to believe you found it necessary to hide the fact you wear a brace." He paused, then asked bluntly, "Why do you need it?"

Courtney had heard that question perhaps a

thousand times, but not quite the way he'd asked it. There wasn't a trace of morbid curiosity or muted distaste in his expression or his voice. He simply wanted to know.

She told the truth. "I was born with a clubfoot. A number of operations corrected the structure of my foot, but there wasn't anything that could be done for my ankle and some of the muscles in my lower leg. They couldn't fix what wasn't there. I can walk a little without the brace, but only for a few steps before my ankle gives out."

Denver strode over to the wide window and looked out at the rain. "You really thought it would make a difference, didn't you?" he said accusingly. Without waiting for her to answer he turned around to face her. "You might not have known me very long, Courtney, but you should at least know me better than that."

She stared at him, surprised and fascinated by the thought that she had possibly hurt his feelings. "As a general rule I don't go around announcing to strangers that I wear a brace."

Denver's eyes narrowed. "I'm not some stranger walking in off the street," he said tightly. "I made it clear that night at Tyrell's that I was interested in you." Her crack about being a stranger rankled, and his anger crystallized into one major thought. "Whether you wear a brace or not doesn't make any difference."

"Maybe you don't think so now, but it would later."

He hated the skeptical note in her voice. "Maybe I should be asking you if you mind my being part Indian. Does that make any difference to you?"

"Of course not," she said vehemently.

"Then why should I feel any differently about you, because you wear several bars of metal and strips of leather on your leg? I'm part Indian, and you wear a brace. Both conditions are what we were born with and can't be changed."

"It's not the same thing. Your ancestry doesn't interfere with day-to-day activities. There are a number of things I can't do that most people take for granted. A few minutes ago you purposely slowed your stride in order to walk with me back to the house. You can't imagine the adjustments you would have to make if we did go out together. Dancing the funky chicken is definitely out," she said facetiously. "So is playing tennis or most other athletic activities. A simple walk in the park would take twice as long. You're a very physical man, Denver. I would hold you back from doing the things you want to do, and eventually you would resent me for it."

He studied her uptilted chin, the defiant light in her eyes. She was even more defensive than she'd been the night he first met her. There had to be a stronger reason than the one she was giving him, and he had a gut feeling he knew what it was.

"Who was he?" he asked, wanting to know whose sins he was paying for.

The unexpected question caught her off guard. "Who?"

"The bastard who convinced you the brace makes you less of a woman. Who was he?"

For a few seconds she stared at him. "It doesn't matter who he was," she murmured, inadvertently admitting Denver had guessed correctly. "He was right about my not being able to keep up. I've accepted it. Now you have to as well."

Denver wouldn't accept any situation if it meant he couldn't see her again. He vowed silently to find out more about the man who had hurt her, but it would have to wait until Courtney had learned to trust him. Whoever the jerk was, he deserved to be drawn and quartered for making her feel inadequate as a woman.

"Why didn't you tell me about the brace that night at Tyrell's?" he asked. "You didn't plan on going out with me anyway. Since you think it would make a difference, telling me about the brace would have been a way to ensure I didn't bother you anymore."

"It wasn't necessary."

His rueful smile acknowledged the point. "That's true. You got rid of me by running away." He took a step toward her, then stopped. He wanted to persuade her to believe him, but didn't want to confuse the issue by touching her. "Courtney, the brace doesn't matter. I don't see why you couldn't have told me."

Her gaze was direct, her voice steady. "If it doesn't matter, why should I have told you?"

Her convoluted logic only added to the frustration inside him. Closing the distance between them, he pulled her into his arms. As he lowered his head, he muttered, "To hell with it. This is what matters."

His mouth opened over hers, devouring her with a need as strong as the elements of nature brewing in the storm outside. He made no concessions, allowed her none. The demands he made on her were the same as before, his intent to brand her with his possession. His hands skimmed over her, his touch searing her through her sweater.

When she made no move to put her arms around him, he did it for her, lifting her hands to his shoulders. She took over then, sliding them around his neck. That small gesture made his breath catch in his chest and his blood heat. Deepening his assault on her mouth, he flattened his hands on her back to press her breasts into his chest. At the feel of them he groaned with sensual satisfaction.

Courtney was unable to resist the pleasure rushing through her. The feel of his solid, strong body against hers, his scent, his aggressive assault on her mouth, combined to overwhelm her with the powerful sensations he was creating deep inside her.

By the time he lifted his head, they were both breathing heavily. Courtney slowly lowered her arms, her hands trailing over his shoulders and down his bare chest. Her fingers lingered with a will of their own, tangling in the coarse hair.

Denver met her gaze when she raised her eyes. "You don't feel any different in my arms now that I know about the brace."

She knew there should be something she could say to convince him not to keep pursuing her, but her mind was foggy with the desire he'd aroused within her. Her thought processes had scattered in a hundred directions. All she could manage to say was his name.

"Denver."

If he heard the pleading note in her voice, he

gave no sign of it. "We need to find out what this is between us. I still want to get to know you. I want you to get to know me. All that takes time. That's what I'm asking for. Time."

It wasn't all he wanted, he admitted silently, but it would be a start.

Courtney searched his eyes, wanting to believe him, but still wary. When Philip had rejected her, she'd been badly hurt and disillusioned. It was possible she could be hurt even worse if Denver eventually did the same. From the first moment they'd met, she'd felt a spark between them, sizzling and crackling in the air around them. That was why she had tried to discourage him from the moment she'd met him, she realized.

Now he was asking for her to recognize that something was starting between them, demanding time with her to find out what it was. She was going to have to give him an answer. The problem was, she didn't know what it was going to be. She should say no. So why wasn't she, she wondered frantically?

She was discovering it was harder to put out a raging fire once it started, than it was to prevent the flames in the first place.

The sound of Brownie clearing her throat forced Courtney to look toward the doorway. The housekeeper was holding Denver's dry shirt by the collar.

Courtney dropped her hands and stepped back awkwardly. "What is it, Brownie?"

"Mr. Sierra's shirt is dry."

Denver walked over to the housekeeper and took his shirt, thanking her for drying it as he slipped it on.

Brownie acknowledged his thanks with a nod, then turned her attention back to Courtney. "Will Mr. Sierra be staying to dine with you?"

Denver's gaze never left Courtney's face as he tucked his shirt into the waistband of his jeans. He could see the inner battle she was waging from the expression in her eyes. Her hesitation gave him encouragement he badly needed. He had expected her to say no automatically. This round was up to her. There was no way he was going to give up, but he would back off for now, if that was what she wanted.

"I had planned on just having a salad for dinner," she finally said as she met his solemn gaze. "If you don't mind eating a light meal, you're welcome to stay."

"A salad would be fine," he said without any trace of the triumph he was feeling. He would gladly gnaw on an old boot if it meant she was accepting him into her life. That admission should have scared the hell out of him, but oddly enough it didn't.

Courtney turned to Brownie. "It looks like we'll be having company for dinner."

The housekeeper nodded. "I'll serve the salads in ten minutes in the dining room. Perhaps Mr. Sierra would care for a drink while you're waiting."

Courtney smiled, glancing at Denver after Brownie returned to the kitchen. "You're being honored. We rarely use the dining room. Would you like a drink?"

"Scotch if you have it. On ice, a little water."

She walked over to a tall cabinet Denver hadn't noticed before. He watched her graceful movements as she opened the doors to reveal a number of decanters sitting on a shelf above a variety of crystal glasses. To one side a faucet was attached to a sink recessed into the counter. Underneath the waist-high shelf of glasses was a small refrigerator, which she opened to remove some ice. The back of the cabinet was mirrored, enabling him to see her face as she poured Scotch over the ice in the glass, then added a dash of water.

He accepted the glass from her. "That's quite a setup," he drawled, glancing again at the cabinet. "You obviously entertain a great deal. I have a bottle of bourbon for Phoenix and a bottle of Scotch for me that I keep in the cupboard over the refrigerator."

She returned to the cabinet and poured herself a soft drink. "Tyrell bought this cabinet for Amethyst as an incentive for her to entertain more. Momma's idea of entertaining is to hand out beers and soft drinks, and to throw some hot dogs and hamburgers on a grill and let everyone help themselves. Her house in Nashville already has a bar, and Amber and Crystal both live in condos in Nashville where there's barely enough room for all their clothes. I ended up with this because I have the room for it, and Momma didn't want to hurt Tyrell's feelings by refusing his gift."

Denver raised his glass to clink it with hers. His eyes were serious as he gazed down at her. "To beginnings, not endings."

"To the present, not the future."

He grinned. "Is that your subtle way of telling me our relationship doesn't have a future?"

"We've only seen each other three times and

talked on the phone once. I hardly call that a basis for a relationship." Changing the subject, she asked, "Did your brother really glue your cup to your desk?"

Denver enjoyed the glitter of amusement in her eyes. "I'm afraid so. Phoenix is a bit of a practical joker. He has absolutely no shame. I've had my shoes nailed to the floor, worn a sign on my back at a construction site that said, 'Hug me, I'm lonely,' and tried to slip on a jacket after he'd stapled the sleeves shut."

"What do you do about it?"

He shrugged. "Yell mostly. I don't have his imagination, or I'd pay him back in his own way." A gleam of interest entered his eyes. "You wouldn't happen to know any good practical jokes, would you?"

"Sorry."

"It was just a thought. So who's this guy who gave you such a hard time?"

She blinked and frowned. "What guy?"

"The one who convinced you your brace is a problem."

She set her glass down carefully. "I made a fool of myself a few years ago. I didn't enjoy the experience. Why would I want to talk about it?"

"I like to know what I'm up against. I can't fight a battle unless I know who my enemy is."

She needed to end this particular conversation once and for all, Courtney thought. "I believed I was in love with a man, and I believed he loved me. I was wrong on both counts."

"What happened?"

She was saved from answering by Brownie, who

stepped into the room to announce Courtney had a phone call from her mother.

"Thanks, Brownie. I'll take it in the study."

Murmuring "Excuse me" to Denver, Courtney walked to a set of closed double doors at the other end of the room. Leaving the doors open behind her, she crossed the study to a desk and picked up a dark green phone. "Hello, Momma," she said as she stepped around the desk.

As she sat down in the leather chair, she saw Denver had followed her. While she listened to her mother telling her she was leaving for Nashville, Courtney's gaze remained on Denver. He wandered over to the bookshelves covering an entire wall from floor to ceiling. His back was to her as he scanned the titles of the books at his eye level, his hands stuck into the back pockets of his jeans. He'd apparently left his drink in the other room.

Courtney knew she would never be able to come into this room again without remembering the way his presence changed the very air in it. It wasn't fair, she mused as she only half listened to her mother. She had made a life for herself, a safe, sane, quiet existence. The last thing she wanted was Denver Sierra upsetting her carefully laid plans.

Her mother's voice became louder. "Courtney, are you listening to me?"

Dragging her gaze away from Denver's straight back and lean hips, she spoke into the phone. "I'm listening. You're going to Nashville tonight, will do three shows, and be back at the Mallory plantation on Friday night."

Mollified, Amethyst said, "Tyrell wanted me to go

to some fancy doings in Texas on Saturday, but I put him off."

Courtney heard an unusual weariness in her mother's voice. "Are you all right?"

"Of course, I'm all right."

"Momma."

"I'm a little tired. That's all. Will you be able to come out to the plantation on Saturday? Maybe stay the night? Your sisters promised to come up on Sunday. It seems like forever since we've all had a quiet day together."

"I'll try."

"Do more than try, Courtney. I want you to see this place. It's really going to be something once all the renovations get done. Which reminds me. I hope you don't mind, but I gave Denver Sierra your address." Amethyst rushed ahead to cut off any protest Courtney might make. "Before you jump down my throat like you did after I told him you were at the library in Williamsburg, let me explain my reasons."

Denver had finished his examination of her books and sat down on a leather couch, his legs crossed, one ankle resting on the opposite knee. Her gaze rose from the tip of his boots to his amused gray eyes, which were directed right at her. He made no effort to hide the fact he was listening to her conversation.

"I know what your reasons are, Momma," she murmured into the phone.

"Oh." Amethyst sounded a little deflated. "Well, has he gotten in touch with you yet?"

Courtney wished her mother had chosen a different word. She was trying very hard not to think of Denver touching her. Or the pleasure she felt when he did.

"Yes, he has." She glanced quickly at the door, looking for any sign of Brownie hovering around, but she was evidently still in the kitchen. "Momma, while you're in Nashville, would you make an appointment with Saul Hooperman for Brownie? She won't admit it, but her headaches are becoming worse and more frequent. If you can make the appointment for the next time you'll be performing there, perhaps we can talk Brownie into going with you so she can be checked out by Saul."

"I'll call Saul as soon as I arrive," Amethyst said. "It won't be easy to get her to see him, though. She has this thing about doctors."

Courtney played with a pencil she'd picked up off the desk. "It might be that she only needs to wear glasses or take a vacation, but I'd feel better having her checked out."

Promising to make the appointment, Amethyst rang off after reminding Courtney about the upcoming weekend.

Denver studied Courtney's preoccupied expression as she replaced the phone. Her long, slender fingers continued to play with the pencil, her thoughts obviously still on the phone call with her mother. He suddenly wished he had the right to shoulder some of the concerns that had caused the shadows in her eyes. The odd thing was, the urge to protect her seemed natural and necessary. The problem was, it was too soon to expect her to accept him into the personal side of her life.

He tried anyway. "If your friend isn't feeling well, perhaps I'd better not stay."

Courtney shook her head. "Brownie would wonder why you'd changed your mind. I don't think it's anything serious. At least I hope not. She's probably ready for us by now."

Just as she had placed her hands on the edge of the desk to push herself out of the chair, the phone rang again. She answered it and listened for a moment, frowning. She started to speak, then slowly replaced the receiver as the person on the other end hung up.

She couldn't know if the person who had just called, warning her about the upcoming history exam, was the same one who'd left the note on her car, but the message had been the same. This new threat had been more crude and explicit, however.

Meeting Denver's curious gaze, she shrugged. "Wrong number."

Denver didn't believe her. Anger tightened his jaw at the thought that she had just been subjected to an obscene phone call. It was the only conclusion he could come to to explain the flicker of fear he'd glimpsed in her eyes before she managed to hide it. He wanted to go over to her, pull her into his arms, and give her the security of his caring for her. He stayed where he was, though.

Glancing at the bookshelves he'd been examining a few minutes ago, he said, "My mother would have loved this room."

Courtney relaxed a little as she realized he wasn't going to pursue the strange phone call. "Your mother liked books?"

"You've heard of alcoholics, workaholics, and chocaholics. My mother was a bookaholic. She would always have a book with her wherever she went. Even while she bustled around the house dusting the furniture or was in the kitchen cooking, there would be a book stuck in the back pocket of her slacks or in the pocket of her apron. She would rather receive a book for her birthday or Christmas than jewelry. She called her books jewels for the mind."

Courtney smiled, as much at the phrase as at the affection in his voice. "What type of books did your mother like to read?"

"I don't think she had a preference for any particular subject or genre." He glanced again at her shelves. "I noticed most of the books here are for research. Not exactly what I would call recreational reading."

"It depends on whether you like reading history books."

"Apparently you do, since you're going for a Ph.D. What are you going to do once you get your doctorate?"

"I'm going to apply for a college teaching position." She heard Brownie's approaching footsteps and stood. "Our dinner is ready."

Denver got to his feet and waited for her to precede him out of the room. As she approached him, he noticed the wary glance she gave him. He couldn't help wondering if she was always going to question the motives behind every move he made.

"I realize these are liberated times," he said, "but I can't put aside all the lectures my mother gave me on how to treat a lady." His hand swept across his body toward the door. "After you."

He followed her down the hall, but before she reached the arched entrance leading into the dining room, the doorbell rang. "Grand Central Station," she muttered as she turned to answer the door.

Denver remained in the hall and saw that Courtney didn't stop to look through the peephole in the door before she flung it open. One of these days, and real soon, he'd have a little chat with her about taking necessary precautions before answering the door. There was the chance she might take exception to his suggestions. In fact, he could almost guarantee she would tell him she could take care of herself.

Courtney stepped out of the way as her sister, Crystal, swept into the foyer. "I took a chance you'd be home," Crystal said. "I can't stay but a minute. I forgot to get your jean jacket when I was here the other day. I'm going to be working on our outfits for the video during the next couple of days, so I'll do yours at the same time."

"I'll get it for you." After shutting the door Courtney drew Crystal's attention to Denver, who was leaning lazily against the wall. "Keep Denver company, will you? I'll only be a minute."

Denver's gaze followed Courtney down the hallway until she disappeared into her room. Then he turned his head and met Crystal's blatantly suspicious stare.

"First Amber, now Courtney," she said. Her words were edged with dry humor, her expression guarded. "Are you planning on going through the whole family?"

Amused, he shook his head. "Nope. You're safe. Amber was business. Courtney isn't."

She walked purposely toward him, stopping a

few feet away. "I don't suppose you would answer me if I asked you why you're interested in Courtney?"

"Probably not."

Tilting her head to one side, Courtney's sister studied him for a long moment. "You could hurt her."

He had already gathered that for himself and gave Crystal what reassurance he could. "I'll try not to." A second later he added, "Don't you think Courtney can take care of herself by now?"

"That's not the point."

"I think that's the whole point. Getting involved with me is her choice to make, not yours or anyone else's."

Courtney came back carrying the denim jacket she'd worn when he'd seen her in the library. As she handed it to Crystal, she said, "We were about to have dinner. Would you like to join us?"

"Not tonight. I want to get to work on our jackets. Momma's leaving for Nashville, so I'll have the house to myself. It's great that she's turned over practically the entire third floor to Amber and me to use when we're visiting." She glanced at Denver. "Momma said you were going to start the renovations on Monday."

"Only on the first floor. I promised her we would leave the bedrooms on the third floor until later. You all can still stay there without too much inconvenience for a while."

"Good. It took me hours to drag all the sewing equipment I just bought to leave here up those stairs. I'd rather not have to move it again anytime soon." She reached out and hugged Courtney. "I gotta go. Will we see you this weekend? Momma will be back by then."

Walking with Crystal to the door, Courtney replied, "I told her I would try."

Just before she left, Crystal looked back at Denver, sending him a silent warning; then she made a quick exit.

"You must be about starved by now," Courtney said as she walked back to him. "Would you like to get your drink before we sit down?"

He shook his head. Walking beside her into the dining room, he glanced at the table where two place settings had been arranged at one end. "Isn't your friend going to eat with us?"

"Evidently not. Please be seated. I'll go check with Brownie in the kitchen."

She returned a few minutes later carrying a plate of cold cuts and a glass bowl almost overflowing with a green salad. "Brownie evidently thought you might not be satisfied with a simple salad, so she fixed a plate of cold cuts for you."

Denver wasn't seated at the table as she'd expected. He was standing with his hands on the back of one of the chairs, waiting for her. After she set the bowl and plate down, he pulled out the chair, then grinned at her when she hesitated.

"Phoenix is the practical joker, not me. I won't pull it out from under you. I promise."

"It isn't that. I don't know many men who hold chairs for women anymore."

"They would if they'd had a mother like mine."

Still, she hesitated. "Would you like something to drink? I could open a bottle of wine."

"I'm not much on wine." He flicked a glance at

the goblets of ice water the housekeeper had set near each plate. "The water is fine. Are you going to eventually sit down, or am I supposed to eat standing up?"

Once she was seated to his satisfaction, he took the other chair, then handed her the salad. "What is Crystal going to do with your jacket?"

"She designs all the various outfits she and Amber wear for their stage appearances. She showed me the sketch for the jackets she's making for a music video they have scheduled next week, and after I told her I thought they were the best designs she'd ever done, she insisted on making one for me." She chuckled. "I don't know where I'd ever wear it. There will be patches of different material, fringe, rhinestones, and whatever else she decides to throw on it."

Courtney might not know what she was going to do with the flashy jacket, Denver mused, but it was obvious she was going to enjoy having it. He contemplated how interesting it was going to be to explore the woman she kept hidden under the conservative front she presented to the world.

After she had placed some of the salad on her plate, he helped himself. "This is a question I asked you once before, but you never really answered it. Why haven't you joined the rest of your family on stage?"

"I'm not the show-business type."

Stabbing a slice of radish on his fork, he grinned at her. "Can't carry a tune?"

"I can carry it," she said dryly. "It's setting it down in front of crowds of people that gives me nightmares."

He fixed his attention on his food. "I thought maybe you didn't want to be on stage because of your brace."

Courtney nearly choked on the bite of lettuce she'd just taken. Denver reached over and calmly patted her on the back until she managed to catch her breath. Most people tactfully ignored her brace once their curiosity had been satisfied. She should have known Denver Sierra wouldn't behave like most people.

Instead of giving him a throwaway answer, as she usually did, she spoke honestly. "I've had enough sympathy, pity, and special treatment to last two lifetimes. After seeing how reporters latch onto every aspect of my mother's and my sisters' lives, I can imagine what they would do with a singer who wears a brace."

"It depends on your voice," he said with a teasing smile. "Maybe your singing would cause more sympathy than your brace."

She was amazed he was discussing the taboo topic so easily and lightly. He made it seem natural to include her brace in the conversation.

"I don't like to be treated as though I'm some sort of freak. I'm no different from anyone else inside."

"Yes, you are," he said quietly. "I've never met anyone remotely like you before. And I'm not talking about your brace."

The sudden shift from casual to intense snatched her breath away. When she found it again, she said his name as a warning.

"Denver."

His dinner forgotten, he reached over and covered her hand with his. "Since we've managed to eat one meal together without anything horrible happening to either of us, let's try it again tomorrow night."

"I can't."

He rubbed his thumb across the back of her hand. "You mean you won't," he said gently.

"I can't." She hoped he didn't hear the regret she was afraid was in her voice. "I'm giving final exams tomorrow that have to be corrected. Then there are report cards to fill out before school lets out on Thursday."

"Friday night then."

She should tell him no. And it should be easy to say. Lord knows she'd said it often enough before when some man had wanted a date. But she couldn't say it to Denver.

Releasing her hand, he leaned back in his chair. "Don't tell me the daughter of Amethyst Rand would be afraid to go out with a mere man."

"I'm not afraid," she said with spirit. "I just don't think we should get involved."

"It's too late. You might as well give in gracefully. What could possibly happen in one night?"

Against her better judgment Courtney muttered, "All right. Friday night."

Denver hadn't been aware he was holding his breath until she finally said she'd see him again. Sighing silently with relief, he stood and drew her out of her chair. Without any warning he kissed her with devastating hunger.

Because their relationship was too new, too fragile, to take a chance of ruining it by going too fast, he forced himself to raise his head before he lost control.

"I'd better go while I still can," he murmured. Taking her hand, he urged her along with him toward the door. His fingers tightened around hers as he met her confused gaze. "Seven o'clock okay?"

Courtney nodded slowly, wondering if she'd just made the biggest mistake of her life.

As though aware of her uncertainty, he lowered his head and captured her mouth in a brief, hard kiss, reminding her of what they had between them.

"I'll see you Friday night," he said, his voice slightly rough, then yanked open the door and walked quickly away from her.

Five

During the next three days Courtney was busy
giving final exams, grading papers, filling out
report cards, and clearing out her desk. Except for
one incident the day she'd given the final exam,
the end of the school year was routine and uneventful. An apple with a switchblade stuck
through it sitting on her desk that morning was
apparently another warning. She'd pulled the
knife out, closed the blade, and stuck it into her
purse until she could figure out what to do with it.

As the students from each of her classes trickled
into the classroom, she'd examined every face in
an attempt to determine who might be feeling
desperate enough about his or her grade to resort
to such drastic threats. A few looked disgruntled,
others bored, some not at all bothered about the
upcoming exam. All their reactions were fairly
typical.

As her last class of seniors bent over the test,

Courtney debated reporting the incident to the principal, along with the note on her car and the phone call, but then decided to dismiss them. The threats would end with this exam.

She did have a few ideas about who the guilty party could be. There were several borderline students in each class every school year, whose grades on the final test would determine whether they passed or not.

As the students took the exam, she mentally went over the list of failing students in her head, trying to figure out which one would be desperate enough to resort to scare tactics. A junior, Joe Trailer, had dreams of becoming a pilot, but his grades were barely passing in English and history, which made his aspirations unrealistic since he rarely cracked a book. Sharon Preston was another student who wanted more than she was willing to work for. Dating the entire football team had not prepared her for the college-entrance exams. Senior David Stewart was the class clown, taking few things seriously, especially his studies, and throughout the year his parents had scheduled a number of conferences with Courtney about how he could improve his grades so he could attend his father's alma mater. Sometimes, she mused, parents' goals for their children were as unrealistic as the students' dreams.

Even though Courtney was extra busy those last three days of the school year, oftentimes she found her thoughts turning to Denver. Each time she thought about seeing him again, her anticipation grew. By Friday, though, she managed to convince herself she was overreacting. It was just a date, not a lifetime commitment. It was simply time for her to come out of her self-imposed exile. She was a little older and a lot wiser since Philip. Denver Sierra was amusing, charming, and attractive, certainly no threat to her in any way, as long as she remembered not to expect too much.

It was just a casual date, she reminded herself that evening as she began to dress. She was tucking a white silk shirt into her pleated black slacks when Brownie entered her bedroom carrying her suit jacket, still covered with plastic from the dry cleaner's.

The older woman frowned as she noticed Courtney's slacks. "Is that what you're going to wear?"

Courtney hid her smile. Brownie was of the generation and background that considered slacks improper attire for going out in public. Fastening a belt around her waist, she said, "I don't think we're going anywhere fancy, Brownie."

Brownie's frown merely deepened as she removed the plastic covering and handed the red-and-black-checked jacket to Courtney. As Courtney slipped the jacket on, Brownie stared at her hair. "Why have you knotted your hair up like that? It's much prettier loose."

Courtney had plaited her hair into a french braid, a style she liked. Obviously hers wasn't a universal opinion. This time she smiled at Brownie. "You haven't fussed this much about my appearance since I was sixteen and getting ready to go to my first prom."

Brownie was unabashed. "Well, it seems almost that long since you've gone out with a man."

Courtney had to acknowledge that it seemed

almost that long to her too. Maybe that was why she felt as though a dozen butterflies were fluttering around in her stomach. Time to change the subject, she decided.

"Are you still put out with Momma for making that appointment with Dr. Hooperman?"

"I got better things to do with my time than go gallivanting off to Nashville to see some doctor," Brownie grumbled. "I'm only going because your Momma said she needed my help with packing some of her belongings she wants brought to the plantation. I'll go see this doctor fella if it don't take too long."

Courtney hid her amusement by turning back to her dresser. It had taken some fancy maneuvering on her mother's part, but finally Brownie was agreeing to see a doctor.

After all her careful rationalizations over the last several days, Courtney found it a bit disconcerting to have her heart jump into her throat when she heard the doorbell chime, announcing Denver's arrival. Acting as though the doorbell were the signal for the start of a race, Brownie rushed from the bedroom to open the door.

Scowling at herself in the mirror as she gave her appearance a final check, Courtney reminded herself that thousands of people went out on dates every night of the year. Nothing extraordinary was going to happen.

She couldn't have been more wrong.

When she saw Denver's dark expression as he stood by the front door waiting for her, she wondered if he had been having second thoughts about this evening too. Dressed in a navy sport coat worn over a white shirt and gray slacks, he was even more attractive than she remembered. But he certainly didn't look as if he were anticipating a few hours of her company with much pleasure. She slowed her pace as she walked toward him, trying to come up with just the right thing to say to get them both off the hook.

"We've got a problem," he said ominously.

She started to open her mouth to tell him she understood, when he grabbed her hand and drew her out the door. Evidently the problem he was referring to wasn't the same one she thought they had.

A large black Bronco truck was parked in her driveway. Instead of guiding her around to the passenger side, Denver led her to the back of the vehicle. Releasing her hand, he lowered the window panel in the rear door.

He gestured for her to look inside, then clamped his fists on his hips. "That's our problem."

It took a few seconds for her eyes to adjust to the dark interior of the truck. At first she wasn't sure she actually saw what her brain was telling her was there. She blinked and looked again.

"Denver," she said, stepping back and looking up at him, "there's a goat in the back of your truck."

"That was my guess too," he muttered.

She turned her head to peer into the truck again. A multicolored pygmy goat was happily munching on a bale of hay, completely unbothered by the humans staring at him.

Her mouth twisted into a smile she tried in vain to conceal. "What's his name?"

"How the hell do I know? It's not my goat. I didn't put it back there."

"Ah," she sighed, light dawning in her mind. "Phoenix."

"Phoenix," he repeated. He shut the tinted window, securing the animal inside. "I didn't notice the darn goat until I pulled into your driveway. He must have been sleeping all the way from Richmond, since I didn't see him in the rearview mirror. I was about to shut off the engine when I heard this god-awful bleating sound behind me. I about jumped out of my skin."

Courtney struggled valiantly to keep from laughing. She raised her hand to cover her mouth, but a sound resembling a giggle escaped. Then she was leaning against the rear of the Bronco, holding her sides as she laughed merrily at his predicament.

Whether because of the sound of her laughter or his own sense of the ridiculous, Denver joined her against the truck, his deep rumbling laughter blending with hers.

As her amusement wound down, Courtney wiped tears from her eyes. "Maybe your brother thought you needed a chaperon tonight."

"My brother needs a good kick in the pants."

"What Phoenix needs is a good lesson," she said slowly.

Denver studied her face. "What do you have in mind?"

"Obviously Phoenix knew what your plans were for tonight. Do you know what he'll be doing this evening?"

A gleam of interest flared in Denver's eyes. "He's got a date. But we can't put the goat in his car, because he drives a Porsche. There wouldn't be enough room. Besides, I don't know where he plans on taking her, so we'd never be able to find him."

"Would he take her back to his place later?"

Denver's smile widened as he realized what she was suggesting. "He might. Even if he doesn't have company, he'd still be shocked to find the goat in his apartment. Do you mind a long drive? Phoenix lives in Richmond."

"You're the one who has to do the driving. If you don't mind, I don't."

He took her hand and drew her around to the passenger side. After opening the door he placed his hands at her waist and hoisted her up onto the high seat, making a mental note to have a running board attached for Courtney's use. On the other hand, lifting her into the seat had its own advantages.

After he'd fastened her seat belt, he leaned over to kiss her lightly. "For a schoolmarm, you have a deviously sneaky mind. I like that in a woman."

After he'd climbed behind the wheel, she asked, "How can we get into his apartment? We can't very well pick the lock, unless that's one of your hidden talents."

"We both have a key to each other's homes." He rolled down his window to let in some fresh air. The fragrance of hay and goat was beginning to permeate the interior of the truck. Entering into the spirit of his revenge, he added, "If you can handle the goat, I'll take the hay and set it in the living room."

She shook her head. "I don't think the living room is such a good idea. I doubt if our fragrant four-legged friend is paper-trained. I think the bathroom would be better." Her grin widened. "It would be worth the price of admission to see your brother's face when he comes face-to-face with a goat as he enters his bathroom."

Denver flicked an amused glance in her direction. "I'll have to remember the way your mind works. Does this deviousness come naturally, or is this a one-time thing?"

"It's a family trait."

As they drove toward Richmond, Courtney amused him with various anecdotes of growing up with her sisters under the casual discipline Amethyst Rand meted out. Denver couldn't help noticing Courtney left her own father and stepfathers out of her trips down memory lane. Either they simply didn't feature in any of the stories, or the men had had minor roles in the women's lives.

He certainly wasn't about to take that part. He planned to become the most important person in Courtney's life, not a figure on the sidelines.

About five miles outside of Richmond, the goat became restless and somehow worked his way over the backseat to insinuate his head between them. Chuckling, Courtney wrapped her arm under his neck and stroked his bristly head. "What's the matter, fella? Are you getting lonely back there?"

Turning his head, Denver took in the sight of the goat nuzzling Courtney. His fingers tightened on the steering wheel as he brought his gaze back to the road. Damn, he cursed silently. He was jealous of a damn goat. He was even further gone than he thought.

"The goat's not very clean, Courtney. He's going to get your jacket dirty."

Courtney had already realized that. It didn't stop her from continuing to pet the animal. "That's what dry cleaners are for."

When he heard her chuckle softly, he asked, "What's so funny?"

"I was just imagining Brownie's reaction when she catches a whiff of this jacket the next time she goes to the cleaners. She's going to be real curious about what we were doing this evening." As the goat shifted even closer, she coughed slightly. "Whew, you were a better companion downwind."

Denver had to agree with her. During the drive to Courtney's earlier he hadn't been aware of any unusual odor. Now that the goat was closer, it was definitely making its presence known.

Out of the corner of his eye he saw Courtney open her purse, then he heard a hissing sound. When he turned his head to see what she was doing, he was hit with a different scent, one he vaguely recognized.

"You're spraying perfume on a goat?" he asked with amused astonishment. "How is he going to go back to wherever Phoenix got him smelling like that? He'll be booted out of the barnyard."

Finished, Courtney deposited the small atomizer back into her purse. "Don't mind him, Chanel," she said calmly, patting the goat's head. "He's just mad because he didn't think of it first."

Denver choked back a laugh. "Good Lord. She's

even given the goat a name. Don't get too attached to Chanel, Courtney. Phoenix is getting him back."

"I know, but he's so cute."

Denver shook his head in bemusement. "Most women like boxes of chocolates and flowers. I would find one that prefers livestock."

He maneuvered the Bronco into a parking spot near a brick apartment building and shut off the engine. Leaning forward, he looked through the windshield at the building. The brightly-lighted lobby was going to be their first hurdle. There was no security guard or doorman, but there were bound to be other occupants of the dwelling who might take some exception to a goat crossing the tile floor and riding up to the fourth floor in the elevator.

Courtney followed the direction of his gaze. As though reading his mind she asked, "Do you know if there's a service elevator in the back?"

"Not that I know of. There are some stairs though."

Stairs, she repeated silently. The bane of her existence. This had been her idea, though, so she couldn't very well back out now. "I'll get Chanel up the stairs while you take the bale of whatever-it-is up in the elevator. If you run into anyone, they might look at you a little strangely, but they probably won't complain as much as they would if we took Chanel up in the elevator."

It wasn't so much what she said as the hesitant note in her voice that had Denver turning his head toward her. Then it hit him. He'd forgotten all about her brace, which would make climbing four flights of stairs difficult for her. He was about to suggest they both ride the elevator and take their chances. It would be even easier just to forget the idea altogether and take the goat to his current construction site instead. That way Courtney wouldn't have to deal with the stairs.

Then he remembered her defensive expression, the guarded look in her eyes the other night when she'd told him how she hated to be treated differently because of her handicap. He had a brief battle with his male instincts, which were to protect her in any way he could. But he couldn't crush her pride by insisting they forget the whole thing. He'd seen the way her eyes had sparkled with mischief when she'd outlined the plan. As badly as he wanted to save her from the trip up the stairs, he was going to have to let her do it.

Yanking the keys out of the ignition, he shoved open his door. After lifting her down he led her to the rear of the truck. He lowered the rear door, then stepped into the bed of the truck to untie the rope securing the goat to the bale of hay.

"The door to the stairs is on the opposite side of the lobby from the elevator," he said as he lifted the goat down. "Phoenix's apartment is number four-sixteen. I'll meet you there."

Wrapping the rope around her hand several times, Courtney nodded and began to draw Chanel along with her, gently murmuring to the goat.

Denver watched her for a few seconds, his gaze fixed to her weak left leg. The warning she'd given him the other night came back to him. She'd said he would eventually resent her inability to do certain things, but she was wrong. He couldn't see where her wearing a brace stopped her from doing anything, including dragging a goat up four flights of stairs.

Rather than be caught waiting anxiously for her at Phoenix's front door, Denver lugged the bale of hay into the apartment and set it down in the huge shower stall in the bathroom. In Phoenix's bedroom he picked up the phone and called the restaurant in Yorktown where he'd made reservations for dinner and canceled them. Then he filled a saucepan with water and set it on the bathroom floor. He removed the towels from the racks and pushed the glass door to the shower to one side. As an extra precaution he took the bar of soap out of the dish and put it in the medicine cabinet, just in case the story about goats eating everything in sight was true.

He'd left the front door unlatched so Courtney could walk right in. The scent of Chanel Number Five was his first indication she'd arrived. She must have given the goat a couple more squirts, he thought with amusement. Leaving the bathroom, he entered the living room and found her staring at the decor.

He was so accustomed to the way his brother had decorated his apartment, he hadn't given a thought to Courtney's reaction. Even the goat seemed startled.

Courtney gaped at the red upholstered furniture, black throw pillows, and glass-and-chrome end tables. An incredibly long high cabinet against one wall contained an impressive array of electrical equipment, from a television screen to a VCR to several stereo units. In various cubbyholes were record albums, cassette tapes, CDs, and videotapes. In front of a fake fireplace, which was laid with gas logs, two plump black cushions sat on the red carpet. The only decoration on any of the white walls was a single painting of an Indian maiden standing on the crest of a cliff, gazing out over the vast panorama of desert below her. All she was wearing was a brief piece of deerskin resembling a primitive form of chemise. Her black hair was flowing out to one side, her classic features in profile.

"Phoenix calls his decorating style Early Seduction," Denver said.

"I wouldn't know what else to call it," she murmured, awe in her voice. Drawing the goat along with her, she said with sudden relish, "I've got to check out the bathroom. This might top anything my sisters and I have seen yet."

Surprised by the look of delicious anticipation on her face, he followed her down the hall. "Do you have a thing about potties?"

She laughed. "Crystal, Amber, and I have played a game of comparing people's bathrooms ever since we were little."

That explained the odd conversation he'd heard between her and Amber at Tyrell's party, Denver mused. "Interesting hobby."

"When we were little, Momma used to send us to the bathroom when we misbehaved. She never considered it much of a punishment to send us to our rooms, since we had gobs of toys to play with. She figured there wasn't much to entertain us in a bathroom. She was wrong, of course. We played tic-tac-toe with soap on the mirrors, played catch with wadded-up balls of tissue, and practiced putting on her makeup. We started checking out other people's bathrooms to see if we would want to be stuck in them for any length of time. At one point Amber wanted to start a scrapbook of bathrooms, but Crystal talked her out of it. Now we do it just for the fun of it."

Stepping ahead of her, he opened the door. "Then you'll love this one."

She did. The lights were flame-shaped bulbs set in ornate fake candle sconces on one wall, which was covered from ceiling to floor in mirrored tiles. A round black porcelain sink was set into a brass counter top. Bringing the goat with her, she walked over to the most immense shower stall she'd ever seen. There were three brass spigots, one at each end, the third in the middle. There was enough room for six people to shower comfortably without rubbing elbows. Or anything else.

The bale of hay looked considerably out of place. She tugged at the rope to urge Chanel into the shower stall, then fastened the end to the cold-water faucet. When she was through, she glanced back at Denver, who was casually leaning against the frame of the door, watching her with amusement.

"We could put a whole herd of goats in this shower," she said.

"One's more than enough."

She stepped out of the shower stall and approached him, and he chuckled as he picked a piece of hay off the sleeve of her jacket. "This isn't quite how I planned this evening."

She grinned. "You didn't plan on taking out a woman who smells like a barnyard?"

"Do you?" he asked softly, his eyes locking with hers. "I hadn't noticed." He lowered his head and nuzzled the silky skin under her ear. "You smell like a woman to me. A beautiful, sexy, warm woman."

Feeling his breath and his mouth against her neck sent shivers of awareness through her body. Without hesitation she leaned into him, wanting to feel his hard length against her as her hands slid up his solid chest to circle his neck. All caution faded from her mind as he trailed light kisses along her cheek until he reached her mouth. The moment his mouth covered hers, she was immersed in pleasure so intense, she immediately parted her lips in a silent invitation for more.

His hands dropped to her hips, then slipped under her jacket to caress her back through her silky shirt. The fabric slid sensually against her skin, becoming warm from the heat of her body and the friction of his hands as they stroked her. Slanting his mouth against hers to deepen the kiss, he moved his hands around her rib cage to her breasts. She moaned softly into his mouth, nearly pushing his control over the edge.

They were totally absorbed in the passion building between them until a strange bleating sound intruded, bringing them back to reality.

It took Denver's eyes a moment to focus when he raised his head to look for the source of the odd noise. Helping him out, the goat stared at him and bleated again.

A chuckle rumbled deep in his chest as he looked back at the woman in his arms. Her lips were moist and slightly swollen, her eyes glowing with desire.

He smiled slowly. "Our chaperon disapproves."

She returned his smile, though hers was a little ragged around the edges. Courtney told herself she should be thankful their lovemaking had been interrupted. Her common sense insisted it was for the best, but her body was still throbbing with unfulfilled need.

She let her arms fall to her sides. "I should too."

He tilted his head to one side in order to see her face more clearly. "Why shouldn't you want me? What we have between us is the most natural thing in the world."

Because she could still feel the heat of his body, she stepped back before she gave in to the over-whelming temptation to touch him again. "I don't want to get involved with you, Denver. I told you that before."

"I heard you, but I didn't believe you then, and I don't believe you now. You were more honest a minute ago when you were in my arms. You want me as much as I want you."

Courtney could have denied it, but she didn't because he'd know it was a lie. She did want him. She also didn't want to be hurt again. "You'll just have to find someone else to have an affair with, Denver. I wouldn't be very good at it."

He studied her face carefully, seeing the vulner-ability in her eyes, hating the man who'd put it there. "Why don't you let me be the judge of that?" He took her hand and led her out of the bathroom. "We'd better get out of here before Phoenix finds more going on in his bathroom than a goat chewing on hay."

She rode down in the elevator with him, her fingers held securely in his possessive grip. It frustrated her that nothing she said seemed to make any impression on him at all. He continually brushed aside all of her denials, ignored her protests, and kissed her with a genuine affection and need that left her breathless and defenseless. So now what did she do? she wondered almost desperately. For the first time since she'd been rejected by Philip, she was beginning to want more than her career and her solitude.

When they reached the Bronco, Denver lifted her onto the passenger seat before sliding behind the wheel. Instead of starting the engine, however, he leaned one forearm across the top of the steering wheel, the other arm resting along the back of the seat as he shifted to face her.

"Earlier I made reservations for dinner at a restaurant in Yorktown, but I canceled them when I was up in Phoenix's apartment. We couldn't possibly make it back in time. I don't live far from here, though. I can fix us something to eat at my house, if you don't have any objections to taking potluck. Or we can try one of the restaurants here. It's up to you."

She met his gaze as she considered the choice he was giving her. The fact that he was even giving her one was enough to think about, let alone the idea of being with him in his own home. Where were the warning signs she'd conjured up earlier? she wondered as she realized she wanted to see where he lived. Feeling as though she were standing in the middle of a dangerous swaying bridge hanging over a bottomless pit, she debated whether it would be safer to go back to where she had been, or take a chance and go forward, even though she didn't know what was ahead.

She took the first step. "I am hungry. Chanel's hay was beginning to look pretty appetizing."

Relief flooded through Denver. He hadn't the faintest idea what he had on hand in his kitchen, but being with her was enough sustenance for him.

"I think I can do a little better than a bale of hay," he said as he turned the key in the ignition.

After seeing his brother's taste in furnishings, Courtney didn't know what to expect of Denver's home. She was pleasantly surprised. When he pulled the truck into a curving drive, she caught in the headlights a glimpse of a large ranch-style brick house. He parked in front of the arched front door, then pulled down a small panel in the truck's dashboard. By pushing one of several buttons he activated the outdoor lights beside the front door and along the paved walkway leading to the house. Through the narrow windows on either side of the door, she could see light as well.

She raised her brows. "I'm afraid to ask what you use the other buttons for."

He loved that droll tone in her voice. "One's for the garage door, the one next to it is for the security system, and the one at the end is to activate the antitheft device for the truck. One of our suppliers gave the control unit to us as a sample, hoping we'd buy them for our vehicles. Are you impressed?"

"Very. I'm still in awe of a pop-up toaster. This is

definitely more sophisticated." She paused for effect, then added, "Are there any more little surprises I should be warned about?"

"That's about it, unless you're going to feel threatened by a hot tub." He opened his door, then looked back to meet her inquiring gaze. "Have you changed your mind? I promise the inside of the house is relatively normal. The only switches I have in there turn on lights and the garbage disposal. Okay?"

"Okay."

He walked around the Bronco to help her down off the high seat. Once her feet touched the pavement, he took her hand. She was beginning to get used to his hand-holding tendency, she mused, standing beside him as he unlocked the front door. He stepped aside for her to precede him in to the house.

She had been half expecting furnishings similar to his brother's, until she entered the living room off the tiled entranceway. Following her, Denver touched a switch just inside the door, and several lamps came on, softly illuminating the room. She got the immediate impression of soft beige, muted turquoise, and orange, with dashes of sky blue. The carpet was a light tan, the couch and two matching upholstered chairs a gentle blue, with a colorful blanket woven in an Indian design thrown over the back of the couch. Several pieces of plump pottery were placed around the room, one on the floor with stalks of pampa grass flowing upward. It was a peaceful, comfortable room with a southwestern flavor.

She looked at Denver. "Your home is lovely."

"I'm glad you like it. After building so many homes for other people, I finally got around to building one for myself." His smile was crooked, his tone teasing. "You want to take a look at the bathroom?"

"Any goats in there?"

"Not unless Phoenix had the same idea we did."

She lifted her arm and sniffed it, then grimaced. "I smell as bad as Chanel. Point me in the right direction, and I'll wash up."

Deciding not to take her small purse with her, she started to set it down on the end table nearest to her. But she was looking at Denver and not the table, and the purse fell onto the carpet. The impact snapped open the clasp and spilled out some of the contents.

Denver bent down on one knee to retrieve the purse. When his gaze fell on one of the items that had fallen out, he picked it up.

Surprise blended with a hint of anger as he asked harshly, "What in hell are you doing carrying this around?"

She stared down at the knife he held in his hand.

Six

"I forgot that was in my purse," Courtney said. "I meant to turn it in to the principal."

Denver towered over her when he straightened up, still holding the knife. "Why? Is this the usual equipment they hand out to teachers nowadays, and the principal wants it back?"

She took the knife from him, then her purse. Dropping the knife inside, she set the purse on the table. "It's nothing. One of my students left it on my desk. That's all."

Denver didn't like the way she shied away from looking at him. "Whatever happened to apples for the teacher?"

This time she met his gaze, smiling thinly. "The times they are a changin'." She slipped off her jacket and laid it over the back of a chair. "You were going to show me where I can wash up."

He pointed down the hall. "First door on your right." As she started to walk by him, he clasped his fingers around her wrist to halt her. "You're only postponing this conversation, Courtney. I want to know why a student would leave his knife on your desk." Releasing her, he gave her a gentle push toward the bathroom. "I'll be in the kitchen when you're done. Take a left when you come back up the hallway."

As Courtney turned on one of the faucets in the bathroom sink, she was reminded of an oasis in a desert as the cooling water sluiced over her hands. Like the living room, the bathroom had been decorated with the Southwestern influence in mind, in shades of tan and green. Using a pine-scented bar of soap, she washed her hands thoroughly to get rid of the odorous smell left over from her petting sessions with the goat. She wiped her hands on a towel and glanced briefly at her reflection in the oval mirror. After folding the towel and hanging it back where she'd found it, she left the room without looking in the mirror again.

She didn't want to see the glow of excitement and anticipation in her eyes she'd seen a moment ago. The episode with the goat had changed things between her and Denver in a way that going out to a normal dinner in a restaurant would never have done. Nothing like a goat to banish polite social barriers, she thought, along with her natural caution. She couldn't bring it back now. She wanted to be with Denver. It was as simple as that. Amazingly enough he appeared to enjoy being with her as well.

Because of her experience with Philip she couldn't help thinking she might be a novelty to Denver, someone different whom he wanted to play with for a while. He didn't seem that type of man, though. But then, she hadn't thought Philip was either.

Following the directions he'd given her, she entered the kitchen to find him standing in front of a stove with a spatula in his hand. Three hamburger patties were sizzling in an iron skillet. On the counter was a tray with hamburger buns spread out on paper plates. There was also a bowl of potato chips, another containing pickles, and sliced tomatoes and onions on a small plate. He'd accomplished a lot in the short time she'd been gone.

"That smells wonderful," she said. "What can I do to help?"

"I have everything under control except for the drinks. Look in the refrigerator and take out whatever you want. There's juice, iced tea, or beer. You could get a beer for me if you would. I thought we'd eat outside if you don't mind a few mosquitoes."

She took two cans of beer out of the refrigerator and pulled the tabs to open them. After setting one down on the counter near him, she took a pickle out of the dish and bit into it. She washed down the taste of dill and vinegar with a swallow of beer, then looked around.

Like the other rooms in his house she'd seen so far, the kitchen was clean, neat, and designed for comfort and efficiency rather than style. Instead of a picture-perfect setting, there were signs of someone living there—a folded newspaper on the small table at one end of the kitchen, a grocery list on the counter, several advertising circulars and a couple of envelopes stacked tidily. There was also a book with a bright dust jacket she recognized as a current best-seller. Denver apparently liked to read mystery novels.

Taking another sip from the can, she felt Denver's gaze on her and turned to meet his eyes. His expression was mildly amused. She frowned as he continued to stare at her, the small smile closely resembling a smirk.

"What?" she asked with a hint of belligerence.

His smile deepened. "I have to keep fine-tuning the picture I have of you in my mind. I can't imagine my old history teacher, Miss Frohm, chugging down a can of beer."

Her chin went up. It wasn't the first time she'd detected a shade of male chauvinism in his makeup. "Someone's personal tastes don't depend on his or her occupation. I like beer. It's that simple."

She was a lot of things, Denver thought, but simple wasn't one of them. More to keep her talking than because it was all that important, he asked, "When did you start drinking beer?"

"It's Momma's favorite drink. Sometimes it's all she has on hand. It's either beer, lemonade, or water. Amber and I will have a beer once in a while with Momma, but Crystal doesn't."

That didn't surprise him. Cool Crystal was more the refined cocktail type. "You never talk about your father or either of your stepfathers. Why?"

"There was only one stepfather after my parent's divorce. Amber's father. I didn't see either my father or Fraser Childs all that often."

"Why is that?"

"They weren't around much. But then, neither was Momma. Her career took her away from home a great deal, and one by one the husbands gave up trying to talk her into being a wife first, a singer second."

"Did you girls travel with her often?"

"Amber and Crystal did during summer vacations."

He didn't have to ask why Courtney hadn't. He already knew the answer. She'd been in and out of hospitals.

Dishing out the hamburgers from the skillet, Denver placed them on the buns. "Would you bring the beers? I'll take the tray."

Out back a flagstone terrace extended almost the entire length of the house, ending at a glassed-in structure at one end. At first Courtney guessed it was a greenhouse, since she could see the shadowy outline of plants inside. Sliding doors facing the terrace were open, and she could hear the sound of water bubbling and frothing like a boiling cauldron. Not a greenhouse, then. A hot tub.

Denver set the tray on a square patio table and pulled out a chair for her. Before he sat down, he struck a wooden match and applied it to the wick of a hurricane lamp in the center of the table.

Once he was settled in the chair beside her, he handed her a plate. As he piled a slice of onion and a tomato onto his hamburger before biting into it, she thought of how uncomplicated Denver Sierra was in a complicated world. He didn't set out to impress her in any way, as some men might with fancy dinners and a spectacular lifestyle. Denver was his own man in his own world. Take him or leave him.

Even in the short time she'd been with him, she was finding it exceedingly difficult to think of saying good-bye to him. And that was where the danger lay.

She bit into her own hamburger, shifting her gaze to the grass extending away from the terrace. There wasn't enough light for her to see how far his land stretched behind his house. She got the impression of space, which she hadn't expected. Most of the newer homes were allotted a small amount of land, in order for the developer to use as much property as he could for financial benefit.

As though reading her mind, Denver said, "I bought the lots surrounding this one so no one could build on them."

"How did you know that's what I was thinking about?"

When she turned to look at him, Denver was relieved her attention was no longer on the area behind his house. It was too dark for her to see the stakes he'd driven into the ground, marking off the plot of land he'd designated for a swimming pool. He was ready to admit he was having a pool put in for her, but he knew she wasn't ready to know it.

He shrugged. "You have very expressive eyes."

Courtney stared at him for a moment as she absorbed the low, sensual timbre of his voice, then lowered her gaze to her plate. She didn't like that he could read her so well, so easily, when she wasn't able to read him at all half the time.

Denver watched the way the slight breeze played

with the hair at the nape of her neck. He wanted her to look at him again, not shut him out. "Tell me about the knife."

She hesitated for a long moment, but spoke at last. "Occasionally there are students who try to intimidate teachers. Instead of leaving live frogs in desk drawers or tacks on chairs, they come up with more imaginative pranks."

"A switchblade isn't what I would call a prank, Courtney. What did the principal say when you reported it?"

"I didn't report it." Seeing his jaw tighten, she hurried on to explain, "It's just like the note and the phone call. Empty threats to—"

"Some student left you a threatening note?"

She sighed heavily. "Yes. Under the windshield wiper of my car. Denver, it's not—"

"Did he call you at home?"

"Yes. Only once. I—"

"What did he say?"

She gave him an abbreviated account of the content of both the note and the phone call. "Some student knew he wasn't going to pass the test, but instead of studying he tried to frighten me into giving an easy exam. If he'd been paying any attention at all this year, he would have realized that was something I would never do."

Denver's chair scraped roughly on the flagstones as he shoved it away from the table and stood up. He took two steps away from the table, then whirled around to face her. "Dammit, Courtney. For an intelligent woman you've been remarkably stupid. What's it going to take before you realize some nut-case student is threatening you, not playing games?"

"The student was only trying to scare me," she said calmly. "No one has actually tried to harm me. Besides, the school year is over. The exam has been given. That's the end of it."

"Is that supposed to make me feel better? Just because you haven't been hurt yet doesn't mean you couldn't be in the future. He knows the car you drive, your home phone number, and presumably where you live. Have you ever heard of revenge? People have been killed for less. The kid could be thinking it's your fault he flunked the test, rather than taking the blame for it himself, especially if he got into hot water at home."

Courtney had had that thought, too, but had told herself she was just being paranoid. "There haven't been any more threats since the knife was stuck in the apple. The test is—"

This time when he interrupted, his voice was quiet, deadly quiet. "You left that little tidbit out on purpose, didn't you? Having a switchblade lying on your desk is different from having it plunged into an apple."

"I don't know what you're so upset about, Denver. Nothing happened and nothing will."

He returned to his chair and gripped the back of it as he stared down at her. "What would you have done if a six-foot-something student decided to attack you, Courtney? What if he waited for you in the backseat of your car, or approached you when you were alone in your classroom?" A shudder ran through him as his own words conjured up frightening pictures in his mind.

His fear for her made his voice harder than he intended as he added, "Because of your brace, you're more vulnerable than other women in that type of situation, Courtney. You might not like that, but you know it's true."

She felt the blood drain from her face. He was right, but that didn't make it any easier for her to hear. Her pride stuck in her throat, making it difficult for her to swallow, much less speak.

Moving very purposely, very slowly, she slid her chair back and stood. It required an astonishing amount of effort to raise her head in order to look at him. "You're absolutely right, of course. I should have reported the incidents, then hired a body-guard and locked myself in my house for the rest of my life."

Some emotion flickered in his eyes, but she wasn't willing to try to guess what he was feeling. When he started to step toward her, she held up her hand to ward him off. "I don't need your help, thanks," she said with as much dignity as she could muster. "I might not be able to run from a terrorizing teenager, but I can manage to walk just fine."

To her humiliation she made a liar out of herself as she tripped on a slightly protruding flagstone. She would have fallen if Denver hadn't grabbed her arm. He didn't simply help her keep her balance, but began to draw her into his embrace.

"Are you all right?" he asked.

Realizing his intention, she pushed away from him. "I'm fine," she said tightly. "Never better. There's nothing like practically falling flat on her face to put some sense into a woman's head."

He wouldn't let go of her. Holding her arms, he made her stand in front of him. "I didn't mean to hurt you, Courtney. I said what I did because I can't stand the thought of you being hurt by anyone; then I end up hurting you myself. I'm sorry."

Something squeezed painfully in his chest as he watched her eyes, seeing the battle she was waging inside herself. His fear for her safety had made him blurt out his own feelings without thinking, and now she was paying for it. All he wanted to do was hold her tightly to make everything all right again between them, but it was the last thing she would accept from him at the moment.

She met his intent gaze. "There's nothing for you to apologize for," she said. "No one should be sorry for speaking the truth. I wouldn't be able to run away from someone if they tried to hurt me physically." Her voice became firmer, more determined. "But that doesn't mean I'm helpless. I can defend myself if I have to, thanks to several classes in self-defense my mother insisted I take. I'll be happy to demonstrate if you don't let go of me."

He didn't release her. "I'll take my chances," he said quietly. "I'll do just about anything you ask of me, except let you go. I care about you, Courtney. Maybe more than you're comfortable with right now, but that doesn't change how I feel."

Even though she could have forced him to let go of her, she didn't follow through on her threat. She suddenly remembered something her mother had once said. "When you're so furious at a man you want to belt him one, then want to kiss him and make it better, you're in love."

Courtney's shoulders slumped with defeat. He had overwhelmed her defenses without lifting a finger, and she had fallen in love with him. The revelation stunned her. She didn't know how it happened, or why. She needed to think, to be alone.

She glanced toward the sliding doors leading into his house. "I'd like to go home now if you don't mind. I've had just about all the fun and excitement I can handle for one night. Ending it with a fight seems appropriate somehow."

He shook his head. "Not yet. We're going to get this out of the way if it takes all night."

Before she could protest again, they both heard a knocking on his front door. It was muted because of the distance, but still loud enough that whoever was there must be pounding on the door with his fist.

Mouthing a blunt swear word at the interruption, Denver dropped his hands. "If that's Phoenix with the damned goat, he'd better get ready for a trip to the emergency room."

A few minutes later Courtney discovered that was exactly where Phoenix was.

Denver brought the man who'd been pounding on the door out onto the terrace, and her eyes widened when she saw his uniform and the gun he wore in a holster at his waist. Denver introduced him as Stan Jones. The policeman nodded in her direction, mumbling politely, "Ma'am."

Her gaze went from Denver to the policeman, then back to Denver. She stared at him, completely mystified. His expression wasn't helping her figure anything out. He was trying very hard not to laugh.

"Didn't you pay your parking tickets?" she asked him.

The lines at the corners of his eyes deepened with his amusement. "Stan's a friend of mine who just happened to be in the emergency room at the hospital when Phoenix and his date were brought in. Stan thought I might like to know about it."

Courtney took her cue from Denver. He didn't seem upset, so apparently Phoenix hadn't been seriously hurt. "What happened? Was he in a car accident?"

Denver's smile broadened. The policeman chuckled. Feeling left out, she asked again, "What happened to Phoenix?"

Denver managed to contain his laughter. "From what Stan could piece together, Phoenix had forgotten his wallet, so he brought his date back to the apartment before they went out to dinner." Pausing for a moment, he asked, "Guess which room his date wanted to see?"

Courtney compressed her lips, trying to suppress her own amusement, as a picture began to form in her mind. "She met Chanel."

The policeman looked puzzled.

"Chanel's the goat," Denver explained.

Stan chuckled and shook his head. "I keep thinking I've seen it all, then something like this comes up."

Since neither of the men were volunteering any more information, Courtney asked, "Why are Phoenix and his date in the emergency room?"

Stan glanced at Denver, who grinned and nodded

for the policeman to answer her. "Apparently the woman was so rattled at seeing a goat in the bathroom, she screamed, and Phoenix came running. She was on her way out of the room when he was on his way in, and they collided in the doorway. The woman slipped on some . . . ah, stuff the goat had deposited on the floor, and she and Phoenix fell. She bumped her head, but it looks like Phoenix might have sprained his ankle. They were both getting X-rays when I left."

It really wasn't funny, Courtney told herself. Still, she didn't trust herself to look at Denver in case he was having the same difficulty controlling the urge to laugh.

The policeman held out his hand to Denver. "I'll let you take over from here. Better watch it when you get there. Phoenix is not a happy man."

"I don't imagine he is."

When Denver turned to accompany him to the front door, Stan shook his head. "I'll see myself out." Nodding at Courtney again, he said, "It was a pleasure to meet you, ma'am."

She smiled. "Remember that if you ever catch me speeding."

The policeman returned her smile, then left. Since Denver was simply standing there looking at her, not making any motion to head for the hospital, she said, "You don't need to worry what to do about me. I know you're anxious to get to the hospital. I can call a cab."

He walked over to her, bent his head, and kissed her. When he straightened, he was grinning again. "You'd better come with me. This is partly your fault, you know. It was your idea to put the goat in his apartment."

"You just want me along so he won't kill you in front of a witness."

"That too."

He clasped her hand, and they walked back into the house. As she picked up her purse and her jacket, she remembered their argument. She turned to face him, her expression solemn.

"I'm still mad at you."

His expression mirrored hers. "I know. I don't blame you. I'm mad at myself." He helped her slip on her jacket, then drew her to him. His mouth covered hers possessively, and she again forgot her anger. "Just don't give up on me, Courtney," he said when he lifted his head. "Give me a chance to make it right. Give us a chance."

He was waiting, she realized as she met his intense gaze. He should be on his way to the hospital, but he was waiting for her to answer him.

"All right," she said. "If your brother doesn't murder you tonight, I'll give us a second chance."

He smiled slowly, his eyes glowing with humor and something else she couldn't define. He threaded his fingers through hers and started walking toward the door.

Before he reached it, he stopped abruptly. "Damn," he muttered under his breath.

Completely bewildered—and she had to admit that was becoming a familiar feeling around him— she stared up at him. "What?"

"There's one little thing I forgot to mention that I think you should know."

She sighed heavily. "What?"

He sighed too. "You're not going to like this."

"Denver, what is it, for pete's sake?"

"The woman with Phoenix?" he said. "The one who fell in his bathroom?"

"What about her?"

"It was your sister, Amber."

Seven

Amber and Phoenix. How in the world had that happened? Courtney asked herself during the drive to the hospital. Not that it mattered, but it was an obvious question under the circumstances. At least that explained why Phoenix's date had headed for the bathroom the moment she'd entered his apartment.

As Courtney walked beside Denver toward the entrance to the emergency room, she glanced at him, not at all surprised to see the frown of concern on his face. His policeman friend had outlined Phoenix's injuries, but Courtney knew Denver wouldn't relax until he could see his brother for himself. Even though he might rant and rave about Phoenix's irritating practical jokes, he loved his brother and was worried about him. She could understand that. She was feeling apprehensive about Amber's condition too.

And guilty. Putting the goat in Phoenix's bathroom had seemed like a good idea at the time, but now it didn't seem quite so funny.

As they approached the emergency room, they exchanged glances as the sounds of a major commotion reached them.

"There must have been one helluva wild party tonight," Denver said.

It wasn't a party. It was Amethyst. Dressed in a white jumpsuit with fringe dangling from the long sleeves and from the V down the front, she was holding court in the waiting room. It apparently hadn't taken long for word to get around that the country-western singer was there. Along with the star-struck occupants of the waiting room, there were nurses in sparkling white uniforms, technicians in green operating-room gear, a woman wearing a white smock and grasping a clipboard to her generous bosom. Courtney guessed there might even be a doctor or two in the crowd. She wondered if there was enough staff still in the emergency room to take care of the patients.

When Amethyst spotted Courtney and Denver, she smiled and waved. The crowd parted magically like the Red Sea as Amethyst walked toward her daughter.

Even wearing three-inch heels, Amethyst had to reach to embrace Courtney. Her smile was cheerful, her eyes unconcerned when she released her daughter. "Can't you just see the tabloids with the headline, 'Jewel of the South attacked by killer goat'?"

"How is she?" Courtney asked.

"She's fine. A little bump on her head is all. She's complaining more about the horrid hospital gown they forced her to wear while they examined her. When I went in to see her a few minutes ago, she was signing autographs." Amethyst shifted her attention to Denver, reaching up to pat his cheek as though he were six years old. "You can erase that frown. Your brother is fine too." She paused for a few seconds, then added, a glint of mischief in her eyes, "He's a trifle miffed though. Did you really put a goat in his bathroom?"

"'Fraid so," he admitted without guilt. Catching Courtney's eye, he said, "I might as well get this over with. At least we're in a medical facility in case he clobbers me."

"I'll come with you," Courtney said. "We were partners in this crime. If he's going to be in the mood to clobber anyone, it'll have to be both of us."

"Three of us." Insinuating herself between them, Amethyst slipped her arms through theirs and turned them toward the door leading to the treatment rooms. "Come along, children. I'll show you where they are."

Expecting a minor explosion from Phoenix, Courtney accompanied Denver to his brother's cubicle first. Amethyst left them to keep Amber company.

Instead of anger they were greeted with a broad smile and wry humor, evidently a family trait. Like Denver, Phoenix's hair was raven black, though his eyes were a darker gray than his brother's. He had a slightly thinner build, but the resemblance to Denver was obvious and startling.

Apparently he'd rebelled against wearing one of the hospital gowns, Courtney noted. The only concession he'd made to the circumstances was an unbuttoned shirt and a pants leg rolled up halfway to his knee. His left foot was wrapped in an elastic bandage.

As Denver drew the curtain back, Phoenix said cheerfully, "It's about time you got here, you son of a—"

He clamped his mouth shut, his expression changing dramatically when he saw Courtney follow Denver into the small cubicle.

After sitting up and studying her thoroughly, he asked his brother, "Is this her?"

Denver nodded.

Courtney saw them exchange a look she didn't understand. Then Denver drew her in front of him, laying his hands on her shoulders. "Courtney, this is my brother, Phoenix. Don't shake hands with him. He's liable to have a joy buzzer stuck to his palm."

Phoenix looked wounded to the core. "I wouldn't do that to your lady." He grinned. "Besides, I don't have one on me. It's a pleasure to meet you, Courtney, although I wish it were under different circumstances. I'm going to have a hard time living this down."

Denver's gaze went to his brother's foot. "Is it broken or sprained?"

"It's just a sprain. I'm supposed to keep off it a couple of days. I hope you're happy. Now I'll have to stick around the office doing that blasted paperwork you've been hounding me to do."

"Serves you right. Maybe you'll think twice next time before you go shoving livestock in my truck."

Courtney had to ask. "Where is Chanel? I hope she didn't get hurt when you and Amber collided."

Phoenix blinked. "Who's Chanel?"

"The goat," Denver answered, completely straight-faced.

His brother's mouth gaped open. "She named a goat Chanel?"

"Only after she sprayed it with perfume."

Phoenix repeated the word as though it were foreign. "Perfume?"

Courtney tried again. "Is she still in your apartment?"

Phoenix shook his head. "One of the paramedics handed her over to the apartment manager. She's probably happily eating him out of house and home as we speak. I'll take . . . er, Chanel back to the farmer I rented him from tomorrow."

"I'm sorry you and Amber were hurt," Courtney said, then added, in case he was still angry with Denver for the accident. "It was my idea to put the goat in your bathroom. It isn't Denver's fault. He just went along with it."

Phoenix studied her for a moment, then looked at his brother, a bold grin curving his mouth. "You're in trouble with this one, man."

Unaffected by the warning, Denver nodded. "Yeah, I know."

The curtain parted, and Amethyst and Amber sauntered in to occupy what little space was left. A new fragrance fought with the antiseptic odors floating in the air around them. Amber had apparently reached into the arsenal of makeup she always carried with her and found her perfume bottle. She'd also come up with a scarf, Courtney saw, which she'd folded a number of times and tied around her forehead to conceal any evidence of a bruise.

Amber gave Phoenix a cocky grin. "Gosh, you sure know how to give a girl a good time. Are we going to try again? See who wins the best out of three falls?"

Phoenix laughed. "I'm game. I still owe you dinner."

A nurse cleared her throat and seemed startled when they all turned in unison to look at her. When she caught sight of Amethyst and Amber, her mouth dropped open. "I'm, ah, sorry to interrupt, Miss Rand," she stammered, "but your daughter and the, ah, gentleman can be released now."

"Thank you," Amethyst said. "You've all been marvelous. Please convey our thanks to the whole staff, won't you?"

"Of course," the nurse gushed; then she held out her clipboard. "Would you mind signing an autograph, Miss Rand? My husband's not going to believe me otherwise."

"Sure," Amethyst said, reaching for the pen. Reading the nurse's name badge, she asked, "What's your husband's name, Millie?"

"Randy." With a little more self-confidence the nurse glanced at Amber. "Would you mind signing too? My husband's a big fan."

Once the signing was accomplished to her satisfaction, the nurse turned to Courtney. "Are you someone too?"

Courtney swallowed a laugh. "Afraid not."

"This is Bo-Peep," Phoenix said as he fumbled

with the crutches Denver had handed him. "She's the family goatherd."

Everyone laughed except Millie, who simply looked mystified. That made everyone laugh even harder.

Leaving the emergency room took some time, since the hospital grapevine had spread the word that a couple of celebrities were on hand. Denver tried to assist his brother through the crowds as well as keep Courtney at his side, so she wasn't trampled underfoot.

The three of them finally managed to get outside, leaving Amethyst and Amber in the midst of their fans. Denver held the door open, and Courtney walked ahead of Phoenix to give him room to maneuver the crutches. For the first time Phoenix noticed her limp.

He glanced down at her foot, then up at her face. "What is this, an epidemic? You're limping. Are you one of the walking wounded too?"

Without thinking Courtney gave him a flip reply. "Just sympathy pains."

Denver shot her a sharp look, but clamped his mouth shut. Later, he thought grimly. They would talk later. "You two wait here. I'll bring the Bronco around."

As he turned away, Courtney stopped him. "I won't be here when you come back. I'm going home with Momma and Amber."

He froze, staring at her for a long moment. "Why?"

Evidently Phoenix had heard that particular hard note in Denver's voice before, because he awkwardly hobbled a safe distance away.

She stood her ground as Denver stepped closer to her, standing only a few intimidating inches away. "You have enough to contend with tonight without having to drive me back to Yorktown. I'll spend what's left of the night at the plantation. Phoenix needs you right now."

Denver had a few needs of his own, and they all revolved around her, but he mentioned only one of them. "We need to talk. We left too much up in the air earlier."

"Maybe that's where we should leave it."

He didn't touch her. He didn't dare, or he might end up trying to shake some sense into her. He was tired, hungry, and sexually frustrated, not a particularly good combination for rational conversation. Apparently, though, this was the only chance he was going to get.

"It won't work, Courtney. You can't keep taking the easy way out, running away when things start getting sticky rather than staying to fight it out."

"I'm not running away," she said angrily.

"Aren't you? What do you call that remark you just made to Phoenix when he asked about your limp? You could have been honest with him. But you can't do that, can you? You can't even be honest with yourself. It seems to me everyone's accepted your brace except you. I want you in my bed, in my life, not hiding behind a brace and a prior relationship that didn't work out. The first night we met you ran away from me, Courtney, and you're still running. You hide in dingy cellars, burying your nose in old books. You won't acknowledge in public that you're related to Amethyst Rand. Even tonight you were all set to leave my house because you didn't like something I said, instead of staying to fight. Some things are worth fighting for. You just have to decide what you consider important enough to climb into the ring and put up your fists for."

He grabbed her and kissed her roughly, temper mixed with desire. His hands were hard on her shoulders as he pushed her away. "Let me know if you ever decide it's me."

Courtney was too shocked to speak. Her mother and sister came out of the entrance at that moment like a fragrant flash flood, sweeping her along with them.

"Come along, children," Amethyst said. "Let's get out of here in case one of those darling nurses has called the press." To Denver and Phoenix she said, "I suggest a nice cold beer for the two of you and a good night's sleep. Then we need to have a friendly little chat soon about proper procedures if you guys plan on dating my daughters. I'll get worn out if every date ends in a trip to the hospital."

She raised her hand to summon the limousine parked somewhere in the shadowy parking lot, gathered up Courtney, patted Denver's cheek and Phoenix's, then herded her daughters into the waiting car.

Seated in the back of the limo, Courtney turned to look through the rear window. Denver was standing beside his brother, his hands shoved into the pockets of his jacket as he stared at the departing car. Once he was out of sight, she settled into the seat and sighed heavily.

All in all, it had been a night she would never forget. She'd wrestled a goat up four flights of stairs, eaten two bites of a hamburger, gotten into a fight, visited a hospital emergency room—and discovered she was in love with Denver Sierra. And then she'd been told she was a coward by that same man.

Not exactly one of her more sedate, uneventful evenings.

Sitting quietly as Amethyst and Amber chatted, she waded through the hurt and anger Denver's words had caused, attempting to think objectively about what he'd said. The problem was, it was almost impossible to be objective when he had exposed a raw nerve. The reason his words had hit her so hard was that she was very much afraid he was right. She didn't want to admit it, to him or to herself, but she had been hiding from involvement, from intimacy of any kind, by playing it safe.

She realized she always had. The quips she made when someone noticed her limp were a way of hiding from admitting she wasn't as perfect as she wanted to be. Shunning publicity was another way of protecting herself.

Staring out the window without seeing the dark landscape and lights flashing by, she wondered how she was going to find the courage to break away from the protective cocoon she'd formed around herself. She couldn't even blame Philip any longer. She hadn't liked what he'd told her, but at least he had been honest with her, which was more than she'd been with herself.

She closed her eyes as a shaft of self-knowledge struck her like a thunderbolt. She was secretly ashamed of her disability. She always had been.

Maybe it had started when she'd been a child with doctors and nurses fussing over her. Perhaps it had been the remarks she'd heard from teachers who pitied her and classmates who jeered at and teased her. The guilt she'd seen in her father's eyes during his rare visits hadn't helped her self-esteem either.

The moment she'd met Denver, she'd been on the defensive, because she had instinctively known he was the one man who could break down her barriers. Now they had crashed down, and she felt vulnerable and exposed in a way she'd never been before.

She could either build the facade up again, or she could begin living her life honestly without any false fronts. The first would be easy because it was what she'd been doing most of her life. The latter would be harder than anything she'd ever done and would require more courage than Denver gave her credit for.

Turning to her mother, she asked, "When is the benefit concert for handicapped children you and Crystal and Amber are appearing in?"

"Thursday in Nashville. We're flying out on Monday. Why?"

"I'd like to go with you."

Amethyst studied her daughter for a few seconds, then said, "Okay."

Denver was propped up against the headboard of his bed at one o'clock in the morning when the phone rang. He sighed wearily. If that was Phoenix again, he was going to throw something. He should have stayed with him or brought his brother back to his home, but after the confrontation with Courtney, he'd wanted to be alone.

The phone rang once more. Leaning over, he picked it up. "Now what?"

There was only silence on the line. Then he heard Courtney's voice. "Denver?"

"Oh. Sorry. I thought you were Phoenix calling."

For a moment he heard only silence again. "Courtney?"

"I know it's late, but . . ."

"No. It's not too late," he said as he sat up straighter, hoping he was speaking the truth. It couldn't be too late for them.

"I have something I want to tell you, and I won't be able to get it all out if you interrupt me."

Closing his eyes to try to shut out the pain, he leaned his head back, not sure he was ready for this. He didn't want to hear her say she didn't want to see him again.

"Okay." Opening his eyes, he said quietly, "I won't interrupt."

He heard her take a deep breath, then she said, "I'm going to Nashville in a couple of days, but I'm not running away, though it might sound like that's what I'm doing. There are a few things I need to do there that I can't do here. One of them is some thinking. This would be a good time for you to do some thinking too. You need someone who doesn't have my hang-ups, someone who wouldn't complicate your life with a famous family or a handicap. Someone normal."

"Sounds boring."

"You're interrupting."

"Sorry."

"I'll give you a call when I get back. That is, if you want to see me again."

She stopped, but when he didn't say anything, she asked hesitantly, "Denver, are you still there?"

"I'm here. I didn't realize you were finished." He felt like a man given a reprieve from a death sentence. "Of course, I want to see you when you get back, you idiot. Just don't make it too long. Okay?"

"Okay." Then the line went dead as she hung up.

Thursday night Denver was prowling around his brother's apartment. Phoenix sat on the couch with his foot propped up on the table, watching the news on television.

"Will you stop whipping yourself?" Phoenix finally said, exasperated by Denver's restless pacing. "The only thing you're accomplishing is wearing out my carpet and my nerves. Why don't you just call her in Nashville? Maybe she's home. Go there and park on her doorstep or something."

"I did. I went out to the plantation several times too. All I found was Courtney's dog left with the couple who work for Amethyst. They said everyone was still in Nashville."

Phoenix fiddled with the remote control, changing channels. "She'll be back. She told you she'd be back. Then you can talk to her and straighten everything out between you."

Denver slumped down into a chair, stretching his long legs out in front of him. "Damn!" he groaned. "I should never have blown up at her like I did that night at the hospital. She's probably dug a hole so deep, I'll never find her again."

"Some hole," Phoenix murmured, his gaze on the television screen. "Look."

Denver looked. The news report was featuring a benefit concert in Nashville given by several entertainers to raise money for handicapped children. The camera focused on a group of performers mingling with some children in wheelchairs and on crutches. Denver sat up and stared, mesmerized by the sight of Courtney sitting in a chair beside her mother with a little girl on her lap. Crystal and Amber were in the background handing out balloons. Like her sisters Courtney was wearing a decorated denim jacket, a red silk shirt, and a pair of jeans.

The news clip was all too brief, but he had seen enough to leave him gaping at the screen, even after the next piece of news came on.

He was abruptly brought out of his daze by the sound of Phoenix laughing. "What's so funny?" he snapped, turning to his brother.

"You are. You should see your face. You had that same stunned look when that magician pulled a coin out from behind your ear at Billy Kramer's birthday party."

Denver fell back heavily in the chair. "Tell me I'm not nuts. Tell me you saw Courtney on the screen with her mother and sisters."

"It was Bo-Peep in living color. Guess she didn't go into hiding like you thought after all."

"Guess not." He was silent for a few minutes as he mulled over what Courtney's appearance with her mother and sisters meant. Was she showing him that she wasn't hiding anymore? He hoped so. He could be way off base, of course. Lord knows, he'd been wrong about her before. But he wasn't wrong about his own feelings. He needed to see her, to make things right between them. And soon.

Phoenix was grinning widely as he shut off the television. "So what are you going to do now?"

Needing to expend some of the energy filling every inch of his body, Denver leapt out of the chair and began pacing again. "Did you hear where the benefit was held?"

"Nashville. Earlier tonight. She wouldn't be home yet."

He stopped and looked at Phoenix. "There's someone who would know when they'll be coming back."

"Who?"

"Amethyst's manager. Tyrell Gilbert. Amethyst gave me his number in case I needed to get in touch with her about the plantation whenever she was out of town."

Using a cane, Phoenix levered his wrapped foot off the table and got clumsily to his feet. "You going to call him now? It's after eleven."

A muscle clenched in Denver's jaw. "I'm going to call all night if I have to." He reached into his pocket and withdrew his car keys. "I'll be at the office. The numbers Amethyst gave me are in my desk."

He had the door open, then stopped to look back at his brother. "No more practical jokes, Phoenix. I'm walking on thin ice with Courtney as it is. I don't need you confusing things by pulling one of your tricks."

Phoenix hobbled over to him and slapped him on the back. "I'll behave. You can trust me."

"I've heard that before," Denver muttered as he walked out of the apartment.

On his back was a Post-it stuck to his jacket. It read, "Beware! Basket Case."

The click of Beau's claws on the hardwood floor echoed loudly as the large dog explored the cavernous ballroom. Denver was feeling as restless as the husky as he waited for Courtney to arrive.

It had taken some doing, but he'd finally tracked Tyrell down and gotten the information he needed. Courtney was staying in Nashville until the following Monday, then was flying home alone. She would stay at the plantation Monday night, then go on to her own house the next day. Amethyst was staying in Nashville to oversee the video Crystal and Amber were making.

Denver spent the next four days carefully making plans for Courtney's return and going quietly crazy wondering what she would say to him after being away for more than a week. On Monday he arranged for the couple who kept the house to take the night off and had some of his workmen clear out the construction debris left in the ballroom. His Bronco was parked around back out of sight. The electricity was off in every room in the house except the kitchen, due to some work the electricians were doing, but he had confiscated some of the lanterns the housekeeper had been using. One sat on a board resting on two sawhorses, while three others were on the floor around the room.

The crystal prisms of the large chandelier overhead caught light from the lanterns and sent reflections onto the floor and walls.

His inspection completed, Beau walked back to Denver and sat on his haunches, watching as Denver inserted a cassette tape into a portable player sitting on the makeshift table. He compressed one of the buttons, and harpsichord, flute, and mandolin music flowed into the room.

He glanced down at Beau. "This better work," he muttered.

The sound of a car door closing made him jump, even though he was expecting it. He stayed where he was, straining to hear the limousine drive away, the front door open and close, Courtney's footsteps on the marble floor of the foyer. Then he took a deep breath and slowly turned to face the door of the ballroom.

Eight

As Courtney closed the heavy front door, she reached automatically for the light switch, but nothing happened. *Now what?* she wondered. First the taxi she'd taken to the airport in Nashville had had a flat tire, which had almost made her miss her flight. Then she'd been seated next to a woman holding a baby that had cried from takeoff to landing. Now the darn lights didn't want to work.

Belatedly she remembered her mother telling her the electricity was off while some new wiring was installed. Only the kitchen had electricity, but at least she'd be able to fix herself something to eat. She wasn't remotely hungry, though. All she wanted to do was trudge upstairs and go to bed. The trip to Nashville had been exhausting. Keeping up with her mother and sisters alone had taken all the starch out of her, leaving her as limp as yesterday's lettuce. Accompanying a reluctant

Brownie to the doctor's office and to the hospital for tests hadn't been a picnic either.

She leaned against the door for a moment, wishing she were in her own house instead of her mother's. But she'd promised Amethyst she would stay at the plantation at least the first night she got back from Nashville, instead of being alone at her own house. She hadn't pointed out that aside from the housekeeper and the gardener-handyman, who kept to themselves, she was going to be virtually alone at the plantation anyway. It didn't matter that Brownie wouldn't be back for a couple more days. She would stay the night, then take Beau back to her house in the morning.

She heard her dog before she saw him, his nails clicking across the cold marble floor as he paced toward her. Usually Mrs. Gilly insisted he stay outside. He'd either somehow gotten past the housekeeper, or she'd relented for some reason. Bending down, Courtney hugged his thick neck and stroked his fur as he snuggled against her.

"I missed you too," she said, laughing softly. She straightened, keeping her hand on his head, and noticed the dim light coming from the ballroom. Then she heard the faint but unmistakable strains of a harpsichord. Her first thought was that the construction workers had stayed late, but the type of music she'd heard last week before she and her family had left for the airport was loud rock music, not the romantic melody playing now.

It was also a possibility, though a slim one, that Mrs. Gilly and her husband were using the ballroom for romantic purposes. From what little Courtney had seen of either of them, she couldn't picture the somber couple dancing in the ball-room.

She walked slowly toward the wide doorway. The light grew brighter, but all she could see was that the ballroom had been stripped of all the lumber and construction equipment that had been there the previous week. Except for lighted lanterns sitting around the room.

Then she saw the man standing tall and still in jeans and a red shirt, his legs set apart in an aggressive stance. She didn't know why he was there. She was only glad he was. The problems still existed between them, but for now they didn't matter. He was there because he knew she would be there. That was enough.

Denver watched as she walked slowly toward him. Her oyster-colored pants suit was wrinkled, her usually neat hair a trifle mussed. He noted the tired slump of her shoulders and the way her limp seemed more pronounced. Exhausted, wrinkled, and mussed, she was still the most beautiful sight he'd ever seen.

Beau left her side, rushing ahead to scoot under the sawhorse table, where he plopped down and promptly went to sleep. The strap of Courtney's leather purse slid off her shoulder, catching on the jacket sleeve, which she'd turned up several times. She kept her gaze on him as she removed the purse and tossed it to one side.

She halted several feet away, her eyes never leaving his.

"Don't stop now," he said softly. "You've taken a

giant step already, sweetheart. Take a couple more."

Uncertainty flickered in her eyes, then she conquered it. She placed one foot in front of the other until she was standing only inches away from him.

He smiled and held his arms out. "Wanna dance?"

"I don't dance very well."

"Neither do I. Wanna dance?"

For her answer she walked into his arms.

He slid both arms around her, not bothering to hold her in the classical dance position. Her soft body nestled against his, and he sighed softly as he began to shuffle his feet. His blood heated as her thighs stroked his with each step. He purposely kept his steps short, barely moving at all, not because of her brace, but because he wasn't thinking about dancing. Her arms were around his neck, her breasts pressed to his chest. The stars were in the heavens, and all was right with his world, as long as this woman was in his arms.

"Nice music," she murmured, her warm breath caressing his neck.

"You're such a sucker for history, I thought you'd like some music from the eighteenth century."

Pleased by his gesture, she applied pressure to the back of his head to bring his mouth down to hers. Parting her lips, she took him in, meeting his thrusting tongue with her own. The blatant invitation was too powerful for him to refuse. His arms tightened around her, bringing her hips forcefully into the cradle of his pelvis, and he groaned with pleasure at the intimate contact.

Breaking away from her sensual mouth, he buried his lips against her neck. "Courtney, we need to talk."

"We will." Her voice was almost as hoarse and raspy as his. "Let me be close to you for a little while first. I missed you."

His chuckle rumbled deep in his chest. "Honey, if you kiss me again like that, we'll be so close you won't know where you end and I begin."

Her breath caught at the raw desire in his voice. Slowly she raised her head and met his eyes. Then she smiled, and his blood became molten lava. "Then I guess I'd better kiss you again."

Denver felt his whole body harden, the painful pleasure as heady as the finest wine. She wanted him! The knowledge sliced through the thin veil of control he'd raised the moment she'd appeared in the doorway of the ballroom.

As badly as he wanted her, he needed to make sure she knew what she was doing. "Is this one of the things you needed time to think about? Whether or not we became lovers?"

Her hair brushed her shoulders as she tipped her head back in order to see him better. "Yes, but not for the reasons I think you mean."

"Tell me then."

She stopped dancing and dropped her hands from around his neck, sliding them down to his chest. His heart was beating rapidly, and his response to her gave her the courage to go on.

"It isn't only up to me whether we become lovers or not. In order for you to make that choice, too, you need to know why I might pull back at the last minute. It's something I've been worrying about." Her gaze lowered to her hands, then rose to meet his again. "I've never slept with a man before."

Denver studied her carefully, seeing the vulnerability in her eyes. She made her virginity sound like something to be ashamed of rather than celebrated. He'd already guessed she hadn't had much experience with sex. If she'd known what awaited her in his arms, she wouldn't have found it so easy to stop as they had in the past. Instead of dissuading him, though, the knowledge appealed to the primitive side of his nature. To be the only man she'd ever known intimately was a gift he would cherish, not abuse.

"Do you trust me not to hurt you?" he asked.

"That's what I should be asking you," she said with a ghost of a laugh.

Denver struggled for patience, which wasn't easy when his body was clamoring to join with hers. "I've asked you before about the man who's made you so cautious about men. Will you tell me about him now?"

It was the only barrier between them, and Courtney wanted it out of the way as badly as he did.

"I'd known Philip about six months before we started dating. He'd directed a couple of Momma's music videos, and I'd met him when I was visiting her in Nashville. He was charming, worldly, sophisticated, and showered me with every romantic gesture I'd ever heard about. Flowers, candy, quiet dinners for two in his apartment. At the time I thought I had found Prince Charming, until Crystal pointed out that he never took me out where we would be seen together. I tried to tell myself he only wanted to be alone with me, until I discovered he took another woman to the Grammys. When I confronted him, he admitted he was . . . put off by my limp."

Denver made a rough sound deep in his throat, but Courtney pressed her fingers to his lips.

"He actually said he didn't want people to feel sorry for him if they saw him with a woman who limped. He said we could still see each other, but only in private. When I told him to take a flying leap off his ego, he said he had invested a lot of his time in me and he was damn well going to get something out of it. That's when he grabbed me."

Denver felt fear dig into his stomach with sharp claws. Even though she obviously hadn't been raped, the thought of someone hurting her tautened every muscle in his body.

"Finish it," he muttered, his voice husky with suppressed anger.

"I ended up with a torn shirt and a few bruises. He ended up with a broken wrist and a black eye. I never thought I would have a reason to use the self-defense moves I'd learned, but they sure came in handy that night."

Denver closed his eyes, but the image of her fighting off some slug was so vivid, he opened them again to block it out. "I would cut off my arm before I'd hurt you, Courtney. I want you so badly, it's like an ache inside me, but I can wait until you're more comfortable with the thought of making love with me."

She smiled. "Don't go getting all noble and self-sacrificing on me now. I want you to carry me upstairs and make love to me. If we have to wait until I manage those blasted stairs, it'll be morning, and I don't want to waste any more time." She hesitated, then added, "I just thought you should know why I'm a bit nervous. I'm afraid of disappointing you, but I do want you to make love to me."

He brought his hands up to cup her face. "I'm a little petrified myself," he murmured.

"Why?"

Lowering his head, he touched her lips lightly, then harder. "I'm afraid that you don't want this as badly as I do. That you won't like it when I won't let you go afterwards. You've warned me. Now I have a warning for you. I don't want a one-night stand, an experiment to see what making love together would be like."

She stroked his cheek. "Let's take this a day at a time. I don't want any promises of forever. It's too soon for either of us."

"I do," he said roughly as he bent down to slip his arm under her legs and lift her. He kissed her with all the hunger inside him, feeling as though he would explode if he didn't make her his soon. "I want it all with you."

He strode over to the table. "Grab the lantern."

When she had the lantern in her hand, he carried her out of the ballroom and up the curving staircase. On the landing of the third floor he stopped. "Which is your room?"

It was difficult for her to manage a simple sentence, because her heart was racing like a runaway train. "It's the second door on your right."

He eased her through the doorway, the light from the lantern giving the room a soft glow. Stopping beside the canopied bed, he lowered Courtney until she was standing in front of him. He took the lantern from her and set it on top of an antique dresser. Turning back, he looked at her, and he saw only desire in her eyes, no fear or apprehension.

Somehow, he thought, he was going to have to find the control to take it slow with her. The last thing he wanted was to bring the shadows back into her beautiful eyes.

He watched in fascination as she slipped off her suit jacket, then lifted her hands to the front of her shirt. Her fingers were steady as she undid one button after the other, her gaze blistering him with her heat. He didn't move until she tugged her shirt out of her slacks and let it drop to the floor.

He walked back to her, holding her gaze as he unbuttoned his own shirt. He caught her small smile as she lowered her hands to her belt buckle, making each movement achingly slow and measured as she unhooked the belt, then the clasp of her slacks. The rasp of the zipper sounded abnormally loud and provocative to his ears.

His own fingers shook as he gripped his belt. "This is driving me crazy," he muttered hoarsely.

Her slacks slithered to the floor. She stepped out of them, then walked forward, closing the distance between them. He devoured her with his eyes. The soft white chemise she wore flowed over her breasts, molding them and accentuating the hard tips. When he smoothed his callused hands over the silky fabric, down her slim waist and over the gentle curve of her hips, he gloried in the feel of her heated skin.

Now he was the leader and she the follower. She duplicated each move he made. He groaned as he felt her hands sliding inside his open shirt to skim over his rib cage and down to his hips. He silently cursed the clothing between her hands and his naked flesh.

Unable to hold back the raging desire claiming him, he took her mouth hungrily as he eased her back onto the bed. Raising her leg onto the dark green bedspread, he unfastened her brace. She stiffened, but allowed him to remove it. He ran his hand over her leg, soothing the skin where the straps had lightly marked it. He knew the minute she forgot to be self-conscious and began to revel in the sensations his hand aroused within her as he stroked her thigh.

He lowered his long body onto the bed beside her, his gaze never leaving her face. "Touch me, Courtney."

When she did, he made a husky sound of pleasure. His control began slipping away as her slender fingers slipped over his chest, his throat, his jaw. Then she raised her head and ran her moist tongue over his bottom lip.

"Lord, lady. You aren't making it easy for me to go slow."

"Don't," she murmured. "Don't go slow. I feel like a coiled spring that's going to snap. Help me."

Her plea swept away the last of his good intentions. He pressed her back into the mattress, taking her mouth with all the ravenous demand she created within him. Tongues mated, hands caressed, bodies heated to a boiling point. Her back arched when he lowered his mouth to her breast, the wet material of her chemise cool against her hot skin.

When she was shifting restlessly with unfulfilled passion, he levered himself away from her and tore off his clothes, his gaze searing her as he looked down at her. He tried to slow his breathing, to temper the surge of desire, but all his efforts were discarded when she raised her hand to touch his thigh.

With gentle hands he drew the chemise off with as much care as he could muster. The sight of her slender body gloriously bare stole his breath.

Bracing himself over her, he parted her legs and settled between them. When her hands slid around his back to pull him down to her, he kissed her deeply as he eased into her. She made a sound against his mouth, but it wasn't from pain. It was low and sensual, sending his control to the heavens.

Time ceased to exist or matter as he demanded and gave, savored and satisfied with every touch, every stroke. Hesitantly at first, she matched his movements. Then, as the ecstasy grabbed her, spinning her mindlessly, she clenched her arms around him and urged him on. When she tightened around him and cried out his name, he surrendered to the shattering explosion of his senses.

As his breathing slowed to a more normal rate, Denver managed to raise his head and ease some of his weight off her by resting on his forearms. She looked up at him with glowing eyes and a small feminine smile.

To his amazement he could actually put together a coherent sentence. "Are you all right?"

Her hair shifted on the pillow as she shook her head lazily. "There's a song Momma recorded a couple of years ago about flying to the sun. Now I understand it."

His expression softened. Her name came out with a sigh as he kissed her gently, then lifted himself off her to lie next to her.

"Why now, Courtney?" he asked, idly toying with her hair. "What made you decide to stop running from me?"

It was a reasonable question, she mused, and she wished she had a reasonable answer. "I thought I was running from you, but I was really running from myself. I let myself believe Philip's opinion was universal, that everyone else thought of my disability in the same way. The one thing I have always hated was pity, and that's exactly what I was feeling for myself." She paused for a moment, lifting her hand to his face. "I was wallowing in self-pity until I met you. You didn't let me get away with it."

He brushed a damp lock of hair away from her face. "I knew you didn't believe me when I told you that your brace didn't matter. In every relationship there are adjustments to make on both sides." He smiled. "All I have to do is shorten my stride. You have to learn to duck when my brother is around."

She heard the amusement in his voice and saw the caring in his eyes. He had brought many glorious things into her life—laughter, loving, and the return of her self-respect. Whatever the future held for them, if they even had a future, she would always be thankful Denver had been stubborn enough to pursue her and ignore all her protests.

She made a sound of surprise when he suddenly lifted her off the bed. "What are you doing?"

"Have you ever taken a shower in the dark?"

"It sounds dangerous," she said, grinning as she grasped him around the neck.

"Party pooper. If we can't see, we would have to rely on our sense of touch. It conjures up some interesting possibilities, but you're probably right." He swung her around so she was within reach of the dresser. "You're still in charge of the lantern. I have my hands full."

During the next half hour Courtney discovered he liked having his hands full. Of her. He supported her weight in the shower by keeping one arm around her waist, his other hand roaming freely as the water sluiced over them.

He was amazingly adept with one hand, she learned, as he dried her and himself with a towel, still keeping his arm around her. The combination of damp, warm skin against damp, warm skin and the kisses he took and gave had both of them breathing heavily by the time he took her back to bed.

There he loved her slowly and thoroughly, building the tension between them until it exploded with absorbing pleasure.

Even though they hadn't slept much during the night, Denver and Courtney weren't allowed to sleep late. They were roused from their exhausted slumber early in the morning by an impatient dog. When Beau's persistent nudging failed to elicit the response he wanted, he lunged on top of the bed, landing with two paws squarely on Denver's stomach.

When he got his breath back, Denver frowned at Courtney, who was trying unsuccessfully to conceal a grin. Beau leapt off the bed and danced around on the floor. "What in blue blazes is the matter with your dog?"

"He wants to go out."

"So what's stopping him?"

"A closed door, I imagine."

"Oh."

When she continued to smile at him without making any effort to get out of bed, he rolled onto his side toward her. Sliding his hand under the sheet, he drew her over to him until her breasts were pressed into his chest. "He can chew his way out if he wants to go so darn bad. I'm busy."

He lowered his head and kissed her lazily, yet with an underlying desire that needed little stimulation to become a full-fledged blaze. Courtney parted her lips to take him in, sighing with pleasure as his hands and mouth worked their magic.

Suddenly Denver jerked against her and made a startled yelp.

"What's wrong?" she asked.

He glared down at her. "Your dog," he said with injured pride, "just put his cold nose on a part of my anatomy commonly called the backside." Ignoring her peal of laughter, Denver mustered his dignity as he got out of bed and reached for his jeans. "First a goat, now a dog. Do me a big favor, Courtney. Don't mention this to Phoenix. I'd never hear the end of it."

She couldn't imagine any situation where the subject would ever come up, but she didn't say so. "You got it. I won't say a thing." Her eyes glittered with amusement as she added, "No one likes to be the *butt* of the joke."

Shrugging into his shirt, he gave her a pained smile. "Very funny." As he tucked in the shirt, he walked around the bed and looked down at her. "As much as I'd like to continue what we were doing before your dog so rudely interrupted us, I guess we'd better pull ourselves together. The housekeeper and her husband will be back this morning, and my men will be swarming around downstairs."

Holding the sheet to her breasts, Courtney sat up. "What are your men going to think when they see the lanterns on in the ballroom? My purse is down there too."

Denver pointed to her purse lying on the dresser. "I went down and shut off the lanterns so we didn't burn the house down. While I was there, I retrieved your purse."

"When did you do all that?"

He grinned. "While you were sleeping. You were evidently tired. Must have been from jet lag or something."

"I don't think there's been a single reported incidence of jet lag from Nashville to Richmond."

He tucked a strand of her hair behind her ear. "Must have been from the other stuff. Did you know you make these funny little sounds when you sleep? It's very arousing."

He saw her twist around to grab one of the pillows. Holding up his hands, he backed toward the door, nearly trampling over Beau in the process. "Boy, you're really touchy in the morning."

He was on the other side of the door when the pillow hit it with a soft thud.

Even though she had driven her car to the plantation, Courtney gave in to Denver's insistence about taking her home. She wanted to be with him as long as she could. He didn't like the idea of her staying at her house alone, but when she reminded him of the noise and chaos the workmen were making at the plantation, he allowed she had a point.

After he lifted her onto the front seat of his Bronco, he laid his hand on her thigh with casual intimacy. "When will Brownie be back?"

"In a couple of days. Momma talked her into staying in Nashville until she flies back herself. Brownie's having a little trouble getting used to the bifocals she has to wear, and Momma thinks it will help if she's kept busy packing Momma's things."

"Is that what caused her headaches? She needed glasses?"

Courtney chuckled as she remembered the look of horror on Brownie's face when the doctor told her she was going to have to wear bifocals. "She had every test in the book, but thankfully that's all it was. To Brownie, though, it's a major calamity. We never thought she had an ounce of vanity until she heard she had to wear glasses."

His fingers tightened on her thigh. "Did she go with you when you all went to the benefit for handicapped children?"

Courtney nodded. "She knows having to accept

the signs of aging is minor compared to what those children have to face every day. Still, it was a blow to her ego."

He gave her a quick kiss. "I'm glad she's all right. And though I don't like you being alone during the day, at least with Brownie gone we'll have some privacy tonight."

Desire rushed through Courtney at the thought of being alone with Denver. She raised her hand to his face, relishing the pleasure at having the right to touch him. "Maybe I have other plans," she murmured.

"No problem, as long as they include me. Speaking of plans, Phoenix and I are getting an award from the Richmond Building Association Saturday night. I want you to come with me."

With his hand still on her leg, Denver felt her sudden tension, but he wasn't going to allow her to revert to her hermitlike existence. Releasing her, he shut her door and called to Beau, who was racing around the yard.

The large dog jumped easily into the back of the Bronco. He paced back and forth for the first couple of miles, sniffing out the remaining scent left by the goat.

Courtney was silent during the drive to her house. Denver didn't press her about going to the awards banquet. He'd made up his mind she was going. He had to be there, and he didn't want to go without her. It was as simple as that.

When he parked in her driveway, he had to say her name twice before she dragged herself from her thoughts to look at him. Feeling she needed some sort of reassurance, he said, "I know you don't want to go to the banquet, but I need you there." He took her hand and laced his fingers through hers. "You'll be with me. Isn't that reason enough to go?"

Strangely enough, it was, she realized. She would gladly walk over hot coals, brace or no brace, if Denver was waiting for her on the other side.

"I'll go," she said, "but if Phoenix puts a whoopee cushion on my chair, I don't want you to stop me when I dump my salad over his head."

His grin was part relief, part humor. Leaning over, he kissed her. "I'll even help."

Beau raced on ahead of them as they walked to Courtney's front door. They were about three feet away when Denver suddenly put his arm out, stopping her from going any farther.

"What's wrong?" she asked.

"I don't know. Your door is ajar. Stay here."

He called to the dog, telling him to sit when Beau lumbered up to Courtney. Denver approached the door cautiously, then placed his hand on it and pushed. It opened easily.

He stepped inside, then stopped abruptly. The table that stood near the door had been tipped over, and a plant had been smashed on the tile floor. A coarse, rude word had been spray-painted on one wall.

Nine

Denver heard a gasp behind him and turned around to find Courtney standing in the doorway, her eyes wide with shock. "Dammit, Courtney. I told you to stay outside. Whoever did this could still be here."

"Then I'd be safer inside with you than outside alone if he suddenly came running out," she said reasonably.

She read the profanity sprayed on the wall and looked away, feeling oddly violated. Stepping over the smashed pot, she started toward the living room.

"Where do you think you're going?" Denver asked angrily.

"To see what else is damaged."

"Let me go first in case someone's still here."

"No one's here."

He gave her a sharp look. "You can't know that for sure."

"Yes, I can. Look."

He followed the direction of her gaze to her dog. His pink tongue was draped over the side of his mouth, the long hair at the ruff of his neck lay flat. Remembering Beau's aggressive behavior the first night he'd come to her house, Denver realized she was right. The dog would have sensed or scented any intruder if he was still there.

He took her hand. "Okay, but I'm coming with you."

Evidently the intruder had taken his time going through the house. Not a single room had been left untouched. After checking the house Courtney realized the damage wasn't as bad as it looked. There was a great deal of clutter—turned-over furniture; books tossed out of the bookcases, but not torn or ruined; clothes thrown out of dresser drawers; pictures knocked off walls. The water in the pool was discolored, apparently from having some soft drinks poured into it, for the cans were still in the pool. They could be retrieved, and the filter would take care of the rest.

Aside from the spray-painted messages on several walls, the house could be returned to its previous condition in a few hours.

They ended the tour in her office, and she stared at the several words that had been sprayed on the wall. One word in particular caught her attention. *Your* had been misspelled as *yore* and she remembered where she had seen the word used like that before. While she thought about what that discovery meant, she bent to pick up some of the books that had been thrown onto the floor.

"Leave them," Denver said.

She straightened and looked at him. He lifted the phone receiver and began to punch out a number.

"Who are you calling?" she asked, though she thought she already knew the answer.

"The police."

Stepping over the pile of books, she leaned across the desk and disconnected the call. "You can't."

His fingers tightened around the receiver. "Watch me. This isn't one of those teenage pranks the kids pull on you at school, Courtney. I don't want to even think about what might have happened if you'd been here when they paid your house a visit. It was no social call, sweetheart."

"If you notify the police, there's a chance a reporter could get wind of it. There's been enough publicity in the papers lately about Momma buying property on the James River. It's a small chance a reporter would tie me to her, but it's a chance I don't want to take. Besides, whoever did this would probably enjoy reading about his handiwork in the paper."

Denver's gaze went to the poorly-spelled message on the wall. "It's debatable whether the guy can even read." When he brought his gaze back to her, he sighed heavily. "All right. I won't call the police station, but I'm going to phone Stan." When he saw her start to object, he said firmly, "He's a friend, and he'll be discreet. Yorktown isn't in his jurisdiction, but he might have some ideas on how we can prevent this from happening again. Why don't you go pack a bag while I talk to him?"

"Pack a bag? Why?"

"You aren't staying here." He looked down at the phone as he stabbed out a series of numbers.

While he waited for someone to answer on the other end, he glanced at Courtney. She hadn't moved. Her chin had risen as she faced him, her eyes defiant and stubborn. She was ready to do battle with him, he knew, but it was a battle she was going to lose. He would keep her safe if he had to stay so close to her, she would think they were joined at the hip.

When Stan finally came on the line, Denver gave him a brief description of what had happened to Courtney's home. He kept his gaze on Courtney, his expression hard, his voice flat.

Courtney was seeing a side of Denver she had suspected existed, but had never seen before. Underneath his easygoing attitude was a tough man with protective instincts, willing to fight any foe who was threatening someone he cared about. And she knew he cared about her. Maybe not as much as she would like, but he did care.

Since she wasn't able to continue their argument, she turned and left the room. In the kitchen she filled a glass with water. Realizing her hand was shaking as she lifted the glass to her mouth, she set it down on the counter. She'd been so intent on assessing the damage, she hadn't thought about the hatred that was behind the assault on her house. Until now.

It was unbelievable to her that one of her students would be so angry that he or she would do this to her. But the misspelled word on the wall in her office was the same as the one in the note left on her windshield. It wasn't much of a clue, but it was the only one she had.

When Denver joined her in the kitchen, she was still standing by the counter with her back toward the door. He slid his arms around her waist and pulled her back against his solid body.

"Stan will be here in about an hour. Phoenix will arrive in a few minutes. He was on his way to Williamsburg when I got him on his car phone. We aren't supposed to move anything until Stan gets here and looks around. He thinks we should bring in the police, but I told him you didn't want that."

When he felt her trembling, he gently turned her and held her securely against him. For several minutes they stayed like that. Denver knew how the sight of the vandalism had affected him and could only imagine how violated Courtney must be feeling.

Needing to reassure himself she was alive and unhurt, he loosened his hold slightly, raising her head so he could kiss her. Her mouth was warm, her response natural and immediate.

When he broke off the kiss, he gazed down into her brown eyes. "I know it's not what you want, but you can't stay here. Don't fight me on this, Courtney. I can't be rational when it comes to the idea of your getting hurt. I have to have you safe."

She smiled faintly. "I might be stubborn, but I'm not stupid. I'll stay at the plantation."

"No."

She scowled at him. "What do you mean, no? Where else would I go?"

He released her and picked up the glass of water she had poured. His mouth was dry, but it wasn't from thirst. Stalling for time, feeling as though he were about to offer her his heart on a platter, he drank half the glass before setting it down. "You're moving in with me," he said flatly.

She went still, her face paler than it had been a moment ago. "Just like that?"

"Whichever way you want it. I was going to ask you to move in with me eventually. This just made it sooner."

Courtney stared at him. He made it sound so casual, as though he were proposing they eat at home rather than go out to dinner. But he wasn't proposing. It was more of a proposition. He was suggesting an affair, not marriage.

She crossed her arms over her waist, needing to hold onto something, if only herself. She already knew what her feelings were. She was in love with him. What she had to decide was whether or not she could accept less from him when she wanted so much more.

The sound of the front doorbell ringing interrupted the tense silence.

"That's probably Phoenix," Denver said, and left the kitchen.

Courtney remained where she was, and a minute later Denver returned with his brother. She was surprised to see a look of concern in Phoenix's eyes.

"You okay, Bo-Peep?" he asked.

She nodded, not because she was okay, but because she couldn't speak past the lump in her throat. On top of the shock of finding her home ransacked had come Denver's pronouncement, leaving her shaken and floundering.

Phoenix glanced at his brother, then back at Courtney. The heels of his boots were the only sound in the room as he walked over to her, then pried her fingers from her arms. He took her hands in his, warming her cold fingers.

"Don't you worry about a thing, sugar. The Sierra brothers will take care of everything. We're better than the cavalry when it comes to battling bad guys."

She smiled wanly, finding it easy to believe. Alone they would make formidable opponents. Together they would be an unbeatable combination.

After a long, searching look at her, Denver drew his brother out of the kitchen to show him the extent of the damage. She heard him say something about putting new locks on the doors as they walked through the dining room.

When Stan arrived and looked over the house, she went into her office to make a list of the students who had failed the final exam. She didn't need to consult her class records, which had been ripped to shreds and strewn on the floor. There were only three, and she stared at the names she'd written on the pad of paper. It was hard for her to visualize any of the three breaking into her home and committing such acts of destruction.

She debated whether or not to tell Denver about her suspicions. She could do a lot of harm to the three students if Denver or his policeman friend decided to question them and they were innocent.

She was still undecided when Denver walked in to tell her Stan wanted to talk to her. She didn't look at him as she pushed her chair away from the desk and stood up. Stepping carefully around the books on the floor, she crossed the room. She had to stop when Denver didn't move out of her way and steeled herself for another confrontation.

The question he asked her wasn't the one she was expecting. "Do you still have the note that was left on your car?"

"I think so. Unless it met the same fate as some of my other papers. Why?"

"Stan asked if you'd had any trouble with any of your students." Denver saw her chin go up and would have smiled at her defensive gesture under other circumstances. "It's a natural supposition for him to make, Courtney. I told him about the threats you received just before the end of school."

"Denver, I don't want my students grilled about this. They could all be innocent. This could have been done by some adult who likes to trash houses."

"You don't really believe that."

She sighed. "No. But I want to believe it. I spent five days a week for nine months with those kids. They have enough pressures on them without being questioned by the police."

"Stan is helping us on an informal basis. You saw him yourself. He isn't in uniform. He'll handle this quietly. I promise you that. So will he."

"I put the note in the drawer of the table in my bedroom."

He took her hand, not to help her over the debris on the floor, but simply to touch her. She seemed so remote, and he hated it. He silently cursed the person who had done this to her. She had been so relaxed, so loving after the incredible night they'd spent together. He wanted that woman back. And he would get her back. He wouldn't accept anything else.

Denver kept the other two men out of her bedroom while she searched for the note. It was bad enough that a stranger had gone through her dresser drawers, pawing over her personal belongings and flinging them all over the room. She didn't need to have Stan or Phoenix stepping over her under things and invading the room too.

He didn't include himself in the same category. He was her lover, not a stranger. Soon her things would be with his in his house. She might think it was only a temporary situation, but she was wrong.

The drawer in the bedside table was one of the few left undisturbed, and Courtney found the note right where she'd placed it. When Denver held his hand out for it, she shook her head.

"I want to talk to Stan first before he sees this," she said.

Knowing it was useless to argue with her, he nodded and walked with her to the kitchen, where Phoenix and Stan were sitting at the table.

"Before I give you this," Courtney said to Stan, holding the note up, "I want to say something."

Stan nodded. "Go ahead."

"This note and the phone call I received were warnings about the final exam all the senior history students had to take at the end of the year. Apparently one of the students knew he or she wasn't going to pass and wanted me to make it easy for him. There are three students who failed the exam, but that doesn't mean they did this to my house. I want to talk to them before you do."

Denver answered from behind her. "No. You're staying out of it."

She whirled around. "They're my students, my responsibility. If one of them is guilty, the other two would be innocent. All three of them could be innocent. None of them need to think they've been suspected of something they didn't do. They're only eighteen-year-old kids, not hardened criminals."

Denver clamped his fists on his hips and bent down until his face was only a few inches from hers. "One of your sweet eighteen-year-olds could do more to you than tear up your house. You aren't going near any of them."

Phoenix stepped between them, forcing Denver to back off. "Now, children, let's make nice in front of the good policeman before he has to resort to handcuffs."

Stan leaned back in the chair, smiling at the three of them. "It is tempting, but I think Denver wouldn't mind one bit being handcuffed to Courtney. In fact, he might prefer it, but I don't think we need to resort to such extremes. Sit down, Courtney. Let me tell you how I can check out the students without their even knowing they're being investigated. If you still have problems with the procedure, we'll talk about it."

She sat. Stan talked. Denver paced. Phoenix watched.

Stan outlined how he could make a comparison of the students' handwriting on their driver's license applications against the note. He would also talk to the English teacher about her recollections of a student consistently misusing *yore* for *your*. There was also a basic background check that could be conducted without the students' knowledge.

After Stan had finished, Courtney had only one question. "What happens if you discover one of them wrote the note?"

"We can discuss that when the time comes. There are several options. You could file a formal complaint, talk to the parents, ask for financial restitution. Until then I agree with Denver. You should leave the detective work to me. Where can I reach you when I have anything to report?"

"She'll be at my house." Denver announced.

Courtney jerked her head around to face him. "No, I won't."

Phoenix groaned. "Oh, Lord. Here they go again. Come on, Stan. Let's get out of here and leave them to it. At least they can't mess up the place any more than it is if they start throwing things at each other."

Denver's gaze never left Courtney as the two men left the house. "Why are you being so stubborn about this?" he asked.

He was amazing, she thought. He actually thought she was the one being stubborn. When she answered, her voice was tight with suppressed anger. "Why are you being so persistent about me staying with you? Do you make a habit of opening your house up to ladies in distress?"

"I never have before now." He threw his hands up in the air in a gesture of frustration. "You'll be safe with me. You've seen my security system. No one could get near you. You can't say that about the plantation. The house is wide open during the day with plumbers, electricians, and my men crawling all over the place. Anyone could walk through the front door, and no one would think a thing of it. I don't have your faith in your precious students that they wouldn't hurt you. Whoever did this has one king-size grudge against you." His hand swept the kitchen. "This is not the work of a sensible person, Courtney. Next time it might not be your house that gets battered. I don't want to take that chance."

"I can go back to Nashville and stay with Momma," she said wearily.

"Your mother has enough on her plate with Brownie there and the demands of her career. Do you really want to tell her about this anyhow? You'd have to if you went back to Nashville so soon."

He was right. Amethyst had enough to deal with, without knowing something like this had happened. Her mother worried about her enough as it was. If she learned about this attack, she would cancel concerts and recording sessions and hire bodyguards.

"I can go to a hotel then," Courtney said.

"I thought you'd stopped running. What about Beau? I don't know of any hotel that would allow you to have a dog in the room."

She frowned but didn't say anything.

Feeling as though she were slipping away from him, Denver gripped her shoulders. "What did last night mean to you?"

His question startled her. "You already know the answer."

"Maybe I just think I do. Spell it out for me, Courtney. Tell me why you went to bed with me. Give me a reason why you decided to finally make love with me. It couldn't have been an easy choice for you to make. You had to have a damn good reason to give yourself to me. Tell me what it was."

He was like a persistent jackhammer, chiseling away at her defenses until there was nothing left. Raising her head, she met his intense gaze, tired of fighting her feelings. "I love you. I would never have made love with you otherwise."

Relief washed over him in a flood. His smile was soft and tender as he pulled her into his arms. He buried his face in her neck as he let the three words she'd spoken soak in.

"Now that you've finally managed to say it," he murmured, "maybe it won't be so hard to say again, like a thousand more times."

He took her mouth with a hunger that left him trembling with need. Instead of slaking his desire, making love with her the night before had only intensified his craving for her. He absorbed her taste like a man dying of thirst. The reins of his control slipped from his grasp as she leaned into him and made that soft sound that drove him crazy.

It wasn't easy to be practical when his body was clamoring for release, but he found the strength to raise his head and ease her away enough so her breasts were no longer pressed to his chest. Her lips were moist and tempting, her eyes glowing with desire.

"Come home with me," he said huskily. "I want you safe."

Courtney's heart twisted painfully. He hadn't responded to her declaration of love, but had only repeated his demand for her to stay with him. He was giving her the choice—sort of, in the pushy

way that was part of his nature. She could say no
and keep her pride, or she could say yes and lose
her heart even more when their affair was over.
She had no delusions about living happily ever
after. This was no fairy tale.

This was life, and it hurt like hell.

One thing her handicap had taught her was that
you concentrated on the things you could do and
disregarded the ones you couldn't. Right now she
could be part of his life, even though it wouldn't be
forever.

She dropped her hands from his waist and
moved around him. She had taken two steps when
he asked, "Where are you going?"

"To pack. I'll stay with you until the house is
cleaned up and Brownie is back."

Denver didn't follow her immediately. He closed
his eyes and leaned against the counter. She was
going to move in with him. He would wake up in
the morning with her next to him in his bed. He
would see her clothes hanging next to his, and his
house would be filled with her warmth and laughter. She loved him.

He felt all the pieces of his life falling into place,
which surprised him since he'd never considered
any pieces were missing before he'd met Courtney.
Just being with her filled him with joy. Her smile
soothed a loneliness he hadn't been aware existed
deep inside him. Making love with her was like
nothing he'd ever experienced before, a mating in
the truest sense.

Opening his eyes, he pushed himself away from
the counter, eager to start his life with Courtney.

Ten

While Courtney was occupied with packing a suit-case, Denver phoned a cleaning crew his company frequently used and arranged to have them come out to her house. After they had thoroughly cleaned the house, he would have his painting crew do the walls. He wasn't getting her house fixed up for her to live in. It had to be done, and he had the connections to see that it got done. If it was up to him, she would never return to the house other than to pick up the rest of her things.

When he finished, he went into her bedroom, impatient to take her to his house. She'd changed clothes, wearing jeans now that hugged her slen-der hips, and a white top that came to just below her waist. He caught a tantalizing glimpse of her soft skin above the waistband of her jeans as she bent over the suitcase on the bed.

His body tightened painfully, his desire for her searing deep inside him. The need he felt had been powerful enough before he'd had her. Now he knew what awaited him, and suddenly he couldn't wait another minute to feel her softness around him. He needed to bind her to him, to eliminate every doubt she had.

Courtney didn't look up as he walked into the room, stopping a foot away from her. When he said her name in a voice hoarse with desire, though, she straightened quickly and stared at him.

Her cheeks flushed when she read the blatant hunger in his eyes. She felt the heat of her own passion licking along her veins, and all he'd done was say her name.

He took the blouse she'd been folding and dropped it on top of the other things in the suitcase. Then he took her hand and pulled her into his arms. His mouth came down on hers with a desperate, possessive hunger. He slipped his hand under her top, a sound of arousal escaping his throat as he closed his fingers over her bare breast. If he'd known she wasn't wearing anything under her top, he wouldn't have been able to wait even this long to touch her.

Supporting her weight with one arm, he placed his other hand on the bed and lowered her onto the mattress. "I can't wait, Courtney. I have to have you now."

Her hands clutched at him, her urgency as strong and as immediate as his. "I don't want you to wait."

The need to claim her was so powerful, he didn't take the time to remove all of their clothes. He unfastened her jeans and tugged them down over her hips, then pushed her top up so he could taste her. She clutched his head, holding him to her, and the soft sound she made spiraled through him.

He tore at the fastener of his own jeans, yanking the front open until he was free. Lacing his fingers through hers, he held their hands on either side of her head as he lowered his hips between her legs. Her eyes locked with his as he sank into her, exulting in the way she accepted him naturally, passionately.

She was the other half of him, and now he was whole. Everything else was forgotten as he immersed himself in the tastes, scents, and textures of the woman under him. His woman.

Courtney felt odd as she entered Denver's home for the second time. With a sense of unreality she watched him carry her case down the hall, apparently to his bedroom. So much had happened in such a short time, she was having difficulty adjusting to all the changes. It wasn't that long ago that she couldn't imagine even going out to dinner with him, and now she was staying in his house, in his bed.

She had no delusions about what the future held for them. Once her house was back in a livable condition and the person who was guilty of the vandalism caught, she would return home. Until then she would store up as many memories as she could for the time when they were all she had.

Soon after they arrived, Denver received a phone call from Belle at Sierra Construction, and he had to leave to take care of a minor emergency.

Courtney tried not to let her disappointment show as she walked with him to the front door. It wasn't all that unreasonable for him to leave to attend to a business problem. It was just that she felt strange already, staying in his house without him there.

He bent his head to kiss her, then gazed searchingly at her for a long moment. "Are you going to be all right here by yourself?"

"Of course," she said, because she couldn't say anything else under the circumstances.

"Keep the doors locked while I'm gone. I won't be long." He touched her lips again, then sighed heavily. "Dammit. I don't want to leave you."

She put her hand on his arm and gave him a gentle push toward the door. "I'm a big girl now. You go do what you have to do. I'm going to snoop around, so if there's anything you don't want me to see, you'd better tell me now."

He grinned down at her. "I have no secrets to hide from you. Snoop all you want."

After he kissed her one more time, he finally made himself leave. Courtney smiled at his reluctance. She watched him drive away, then shut the door, locking it as he'd instructed. As she turned, her foot caught on the throw rug lying by the door. After she straightened it, she decided to scout out any other hazards she would have to be aware of while she was there.

When she phoned her mother in Nashville to give her Denver's number, Courtney was a bit disconcerted to find Amethyst couldn't have been more pleased that she was staying with Denver. In fact, she was downright ecstatic.

"Momma, aren't you supposed to be wringing your hands and saying how shocked you are to hear your daughter is living with a man?"

"For one thing, I'm not the wringing-hands type. I've been in love before, too, you know." Her trilling laughter echoed over the line. "A number of times, as you might recall. I think it's wonderful that you and Denver have fallen in love. It was what I was hoping for when I threw you two together. I really like him, Courtney. When's the wedding?"

She didn't want to explain the situation over the phone, so she answered truthfully, "We haven't talked about it yet."

"Well, whatever you decide, I'll be there, even if I have to cancel a performance at the White House."

A few minutes later Courtney hung up the phone with her mother's congratulations ringing in her ears. She wished she could tell her mother the truth, but it was something she would have to say in person, in order to make her mother understand she was staying with Denver temporarily. And why it was only temporary.

In the two hours he was gone Denver called her twice. Each time it was just to talk to her, not because he wanted anything in particular. Then he was back, and the house became a lover's sanctuary, where they could have hours of privacy and pleasure in each other's arms.

By Friday, Courtney had become accustomed to living in Denver's house. She'd even made a few minor changes, like taking up the various throw rugs from the entranceway and the kitchen. The clothes she'd brought with her hung in the closet with his, her toothbrush in the holder next to his.

After they'd retrieved her papers and research materials from her house, she worked on her dissertation during the day while he was at work.

No routine was established for eating dinner or retiring for the night. The first night was spent in the bedroom from the moment he hit the door until around midnight, when a hunger of a different kind had them raiding the kitchen. The second night Courtney planned a picnic supper on his patio, but it was delayed the moment he kissed her upon arriving home.

Except for the snacks they eventually had during the night, they were virtually living on love. At least Courtney was living on love. During the wild episodes of lovemaking, Denver would tell her how good she felt, how he wanted her, or how much he'd thought of her during the day while he was away from her, but not once had he said the three words she ached to hear.

It wasn't until Saturday that the real world intruded. After a leisurely breakfast, which followed a prolonged, tumultuous shower they took together, Denver asked her to go with him to check on the work being done on the plantation.

While he toured the ground floor with one of the supervisors, she made the long trek up two flights of stairs to raid Crystal's closets for a change of clothing. She knew she could ask Denver to take her to her house in Yorktown, but she didn't really want to know how far along the cleaning and painting crews were. She wanted to hoard her time with Denver like a miser with a meager supply of coins.

She had several things laid out on Crystal's bed

when Denver came looking for her. He walked into the room and sat on the side of the bed. "Do you mind if we stay a couple more hours?" he asked. "One of the suppliers is delivering some lumber this afternoon, and I want to check the quality of the boards."

Her back to him, she continued shoving hangers aside as she looked through Crystal's more sporty clothes. "I don't mind."

Denver glanced at the nearly overflowing closet. Crystal's tastes in clothing might not be the same as Courtney's, but her older sister was closer to Courtney's height than the shorter Amber.

"There'll still be plenty of time for me to take you to your house," he said, "if you can't find a fancy dress in Crystal's closet. It's not going to be real formal. A cocktail dress will do."

She jerked her head around, a puzzled frown creasing her brow. "Why do I need a cocktail dress?"

"For the banquet tonight." When he saw her frown deepen, he added, "The building association is giving Phoenix and me an award. The banquet is tonight. Remember?"

She had forgotten. Maybe purposefully, because she really didn't want to go, but she knew Denver was going to be as insistent as he'd been when he first brought it up. Stalling, she turned back to look at the clothes in the closet. Three of Crystal's dresses would be appropriate. But they were all knee-length, if not a little shorter, not the long skirts Courtney preferred.

She wasn't aware Denver had left the bed until his warm, large hands closed over her shoulders.

He gently turned her around to face him. "I thought we'd settled this. You agreed to go with me."

"I know. I'll go."

His thumbs stroked the soft skin of her throat. "Why do I get the feeling you want to add something beginning with 'but'?"

She smiled. He was too darn perceptive. "But the only appropriate dresses Crystal has here are short. A couple of them are very short. All of her slack outfits are too casual."

Denver knew where this was leading, but he wasn't about to let it end where Courtney wanted it. "So wear one of the short dresses." He reached into the closet and took out a sea green dress, holding it up. "What's wrong with this one?"

She took it from him and crammed it back into the closet. "It's too short."

He waited until she brought her gaze back to his. Then he smiled slowly, not bothering to hide the hunger in his eyes. "Take it from a man who knows these things. You have great legs. I've noticed."

Courtney felt cornered by him and the situation. "I don't like to wear short dresses in public. My brace stands out like a neon sign in a dark room."

He threaded his hands through her hair, forcing her to look at him. "*You* stand out in a crowd. It has nothing to do with your brace."

She sighed heavily. "You don't understand."

"Probably not," he admitted. "I've never had to go through life wearing a brace, so there's no way I could know what it's like. I wish what people think didn't bother you—for your sake, not for mine—

but it does, so we go on from there. Still, we can't stay shut off from the world entirely, Courtney. There are certain social obligations we both have that we can't ignore. Tonight is one of them for me, and I don't want to go alone. I want you with me."

He made it sound so simple, she thought. And she was through with running away. Tonight was as good a time as any to prove it to him and to herself. Denver said the brace didn't bother him. She would find out this evening if that was true.

When they arrived at the hotel in downtown Richmond where the banquet was being held, they ran into Phoenix just inside the main lobby. Clinging to his arm was a stunning blond he introduced as his physical therapist, Tamara Brown. The woman was definitely out of uniform, wearing a hot pink Lycra tank dress that left little to the imagination. Tamara responded to the introductions with a charming smile, completely oblivious of the stares she was receiving from every male in the lobby. One man ran smack into a large potted palm because he'd been ogling Tamara instead of watching where he was going.

Courtney caught Denver's amused grin as he took her arm and led her toward the large room where the banquet was being held. She knew that if he was aware of the attention Phoenix's date was receiving, he also wouldn't miss the occasional curious glances she received. People weren't looking at her for the same reason they were eyeing Tamara. The sea green dress Courtney had borrowed from Crystal's closet looked sedate, almost matronly, compared to Tamara's body-skimming frock. Her brace was the attraction, not her figure.

Then Denver turned his warm smile on her, his fingers tightening their hold on her arm, and she forgot about everything except him.

When they reached their table, Courtney noticed Phoenix had learned the same rules of chivalry from their mother. Like Denver he held the chair for Tamara before sitting down beside her.

There was another couple at the large round table. Courtney didn't need to be introduced to the man who had stood up as they approached. Instead of his police uniform, Stan was wearing a dark suit and tie. Before he could do the honors, the red-haired woman at his side bounced out of her chair and flung her arm across Stan's body to shake Courtney's hand.

"Hi, I'm Belle, and I'm tickled pink to meet you, Courtney. I swear I thought I was never going to get to see you the way Denver's been dragging his feet about bringing you to the office."

Still standing, Courtney shook the other woman's hand. "I'm pleased to meet you, Belle."

With what was obviously her usual forthright manner Belle said, "I noticed you wear a brace. Evidently yours is better than the one my cousin Jimmy Ray had to wear on his knee for a couple of years after a car accident. He had to carry a little oil can with him wherever he went 'cause the darn thing kept freezing up on him. We called him the Tin Man. You know, from *The Wizard of Oz*." Pausing for a badly needed breath of air, Belle asked, "So what happened to you?"

Courtney was aware of Denver standing completely still behind her. Smiling at his secretary, she replied, "I was born with a clubfoot. The brace is to give my ankle strength to support my weight."

Belle grinned. "We women do whatever we have to, to help nature along. I myself have had to wear a padded bra since I was fifteen."

That little tidbit of information caused different reactions around the table. Stan actually blushed. Phoenix roared with laughter. His date looked stunned. Courtney grinned over her shoulder at Denver, and he smiled back. When she sat down, she felt the weight of his hand on her shoulder for a moment, communicating to her his pleasure in her honest answer.

The rest of the evening passed so quickly, Courtney later remembered it in a series of vignettes. An unremarkable dinner was served before the speeches began. The only one she applauded with any enthusiasm was the short humorous speech Phoenix gave after the Sierra brothers received their award.

Throughout the evening Denver never left her side, except when he had to go up front with his brother. He found a number of different ways to touch her, some obvious, some subtle, and all possessive and arousing, as was the way he looked at her.

As the evening drew to a close, she didn't need to be persuaded to leave, even though she'd enjoyed herself more than she'd expected. But each casual touch, every intense look from Denver, had added fuel to the banked fires within her, until she'd thought she would burn up.

After depositing her in the front seat of the

Bronco and climbing behind the wheel, Denver pulled her over close to him. He threaded his fingers through hers and rested their clasped hands on his hard thigh.

"Well, little teacher, did I pass?" he asked.

Her mind was on the heat radiating through her veins, not on what he was saying. She asked him to repeat the question.

"Did I pass your test?"

"What test?"

"Weren't you wondering how I was going to act when we went out in public? Whether I would walk three paces ahead of you or be embarrassed because you were limping along beside me?" His fingers tightened around hers. "Admit it. You were worried about how I would react when people noticed your brace. It was one of the reasons you didn't want to go in the first place."

She avoided his gaze. "I know you said my brace doesn't bother you, but I had to know for sure. When it's just the two of us, I've noticed you seem to accept it as part of the package called Courtney Caine. But . . ."

"But you had to know for sure," he finished for her. "I understand, Courtney. Your pride was battered badly once before when that jerk told you he didn't want to be seen in public with you. I can't blame you for not wanting a repeat performance."

She leaned over and kissed his cheek. "I wouldn't mind a repeat performance of another kind as soon as we get home."

His foot pressed down on the accelerator. "I can practically guarantee it."

• • •

The next morning they were having a late breakfast on the patio when the doorbell rang. While
Denver went to see who it was, Courtney poured
herself another cup of coffee. Beau came running
toward her with something in his mouth. It was a
stake of some kind with a fluorescent pink strip of
plastic wrapped around it.

Beau resisted when she tried to take it, but she
finally managed to get it away from him as Denver
returned with Phoenix at his side.

"This is cozy. Very domestic," Phoenix drawled
as his gaze roamed over the remnants of their meal
and the folded newspaper beside Denver's plate.
He glanced at his brother. "I would have used my
key to let myself in, except I wasn't sure what I
would walk in on now that you have a roommate."

Denver smiled faintly, then said, "You'd better
tell her what you just told me."

Phoenix sat down, then reached across the table
and took a piece of toast off Denver's plate. "Stan is
on his way over. He's got some news about the bad
guys."

"Guys?" Courtney repeated, startled. "There's
more than one?"

"It was a figure of speech. Actually, it was one
boy and his girlfriend. The kid's name is Stewart,
David Stewart. I didn't catch who the girl was
except she's his girlfriend. It seems these kids felt
it was your fault they won't be able to be together
in the fall when college starts. Because Stewart
flunked your exam, it gave him too low a grade
average to be admitted into the same college she's

going to. Apparently he hadn't done all that well in some of his other classes either, but for some reason the girlfriend blames you. She was the one who trashed your house along with some of her friends. David wrote the note and made the phone call, but he didn't know his true love had done a job on your home . Stan's coming over to see what you want to do about Romeo and Juliet."

Courtney sat back in her chair. "He didn't say anything last night at the banquet. When did he find all this out?"

"It would have been worth Stan's life not to take Belle to the banquet, so he had his partner check up on the kid last night. His partner called him early this morning with the confirmation on the two kids."

She shook her head in disbelief. "I can't believe it's David. He's always been so laid-back about everything, always joking and cutting up. He's smart but lazy, more interested in having a good time than studying."

Phoenix brushed crumbs off his hands. "I gather he's serious about the girl. Whether she put him up to threatening you or not doesn't really matter. He's still guilty. It's up to you what you want done about it."

What did she want done about it? Courtney wondered. She could understand the motivation behind the kids' behavior, even if she didn't approve of their methods. Maybe if she hadn't fallen in love herself, she might not have been able to sympathize with the young couple's desire to be together. But she herself had moved into Denver's house, virtually living in sin, which was completely out of character for her.

Neither Denver nor Phoenix pressed her for an answer. They discussed work on the plantation until the doorbell rang again, and Denver got up to let Stan in.

It wasn't until she saw Denver walking back across the patio with Stan that she decided what to do. The sun glinted off Denver's dark hair, warming his tanned skin. His jeans hugged his lean hips as his long strides covered the distance between the door and the table. Just watching him walk toward her made her mouth go dry. She looked away, afraid her feelings were reflected in her eyes.

Maybe the men wouldn't understand her decision, but she knew what she had to do.

She was right. They didn't understand, especially Stan, who thought it was wrong to let the two kids get away with what they'd done.

"I'm not letting them get away with anything," she explained patiently. "Believe me, making David go to summer school will be punishment enough for both of them. Instead of having a carefree summer, he's going to have to sweat over his studies, and she's going to have to spend time alone rather than with him. This way it will be up to him whether or not he brings his grades up far enough to attend college. He won't be able to blame his problems on anyone else."

As a policeman Stan obviously had problems with her idea of punishment. "I still think we should tell the parents. His and hers. Even though Stewart's eighteen, they could still apply parental pressure to make sure he follows through with summer school and the girl behaves herself the rest of the summer."

Courtney shook her head. "It has to be up to David to apply himself to his studies if he's going to learn anything at all from this." She turned to Denver. "I just thought of something else they could do as a punishment. Maybe you could find them some sort of job in construction in Yorktown, since it was your crew who cleaned up their mess."

Phoenix chuckled. "You're a softie, Bo-Peep. A real pushover for romance."

Stan pushed back his chair and stood. "Maybe you're right, Courtney. Lord knows I've seen enough incidents when the heavy-handed approach didn't work. Perhaps your way will."

"I want to thank you for all your trouble," she said as she held out her right hand to him.

He clasped her hand and smiled. "Well, it's been different. By the way, your house is almost back to normal. I took the Stewart kid there yesterday morning to show him what his girl had done, but the cleaning crew and painters had everything looking like new." He turned to Denver, who'd also gotten to his feet. "Belle said to thank you for the tickets to the banquet last night. We really enjoyed it. Except for the speeches."

Phoenix took offense. "I was one of the speakers, you know."

Stan chuckled. "You were included in her list of boring speakers. She thought you should have told a couple of jokes. Maybe people would have been able to stay awake."

Phoenix stood up. "You tell our Southern Belle to

watch her paper clips. I'm just liable to string them all together for that remark." Taking the policeman's arm, he started toward the door. "I'll walk you to your car. I think now's a good time to warn you about our secretary's habit of robbing food off your plate. She didn't do it last night because everyone had the same thing, but watch out for your dinner if you go to a restaurant. She'll steal you blind."

Denver remained standing by his chair as his brother's voice faded. Throughout the entire discussion Courtney had been aware of his silence and had wondered if he thought she was foolish not to demand more punishment for the teenagers. His eyes were serious as he gazed into the distance, his mouth a thin line, as though he weren't happy about something. She had a feeling she knew what it was.

"You don't approve of what I did, do you?" she said.

He looked at her. "I can't be objective about some kid who threatened you, Courtney. If he had hurt you, I would have wanted him drawn and quartered. As it is, I think you've let him off easy, but it was your decision to make." His glance shifted to the stake still lying in her lap. "What are you doing with that?"

She looked down. She'd completely forgotten about the piece of wood she'd taken away from her dog. "Beau was carrying it around in his mouth." She handed it to him, curious why he was looking at it so strangely. "Why? Is it important?"

His expression was thoughtful and oddly tense

as he extended his hand to her. "I'll put it back where it's supposed to go. Come with me."

Puzzled, she took his hand and stood. Instead of moving, though, he stared at her. A slight breeze ruffled her hair, and he lifted his hand almost in slow motion to touch her face. Her breath caught in her throat when she saw a somber expression darken his eyes.

She could only come to one conclusion. He was trying to figure out how to tell her he was taking her back to her own house. He'd heard Stan say her house was back to normal. There was no reason for her to stay with him any longer. Even though she had expected it, the end was coming sooner than she'd thought.

"You don't have to say anything, Denver," she said, trying to make it easier for him and for her. "I know it's time for me to leave."

He couldn't have looked more shocked if she'd hauled off and hit him. "What are you talking about? You aren't going anywhere."

"But Stan said my house was finished. There's no reason for me to stay with you any longer."

"You don't think so? Then I guess I'll have to show you."

His fingers tightened around her hand as he drew her across the patio to the back lawn. Even though he was angry, he still took care not to hurry her.

When he reached a spot in the lawn where a small hole exposed the dirt underneath, he released her hand and stuck the stake down into the hole. Straightening, he pointed to another stake about twenty feet in front of him. "Do you see that stake?"

"Yes, I see it," Courtney answered, completely baffled.

He turned, his arm rising in a parallel line to the patio. "Do you also see that one?"

"Yes." This time she was the one who pointed. "There's another one over there."

He cupped her face, bringing her gaze back to his. "I'm having a swimming pool put in for you," he said, his voice low and intense. "It's the only thing your house has that mine doesn't. There's plenty of room for Brownie if she wants to live with us. Beau's already happy here." He took a deep breath, as though preparing himself for a long dive off a high cliff. "I don't want you to go back to your house. I want you to live with me."

"For how long?" she asked, surprised she could even speak.

He looked stunned. "For the rest of your life, of course. What did you think I meant?"

"I don't know what I think," she said slowly. She saw his eyes take on a wounded look, as though she had hurt him in some way she couldn't fathom. "Denver, why do you want me to live with you? I need to know. I love you and I would do anything for you, but I'm not sure I could just live with you if all I am is someone to warm your bed."

She watched in fascination as the expression in his eyes softened, as his lips slowly formed the smile she loved. He shook his head in wonderment. "I thought you knew."

"All I know is I've never been so confused or so happy as I've been these last couple of days, and so miserable when I thought I was going to have to leave you."

He threaded his fingers through her hair and lowered his head. Against her lips he said softly, "I love you, Emerald Courtney Caine. The first night I met you, I wanted you to change your name to Emerald Courtney Sierra and be with me for the rest of our lives."

Her face became radiant with joy, and she flung her arms around his neck, nearly overbalancing him. She crushed his lips under hers, hardly aware of him picking her up and whirling her around and around as she kissed him.

"Can I take that as a yes?" he asked when he let her stand again.

"Yes," she said, her eyes glowing with happiness.

"It's a good thing you said yes," he murmured as he lowered his head again. "I wasn't going to accept any other answer."

He kissed her slowly, deeply, his arms enfolding her as though she were the most precious thing in the world.

Neither one of them were aware of Beau trotting over to the stake Denver had just replaced in the ground. He clamped his teeth around it and brought it back to them, dropping it on the grass near their feet. He was going to have a long wait before either of them noticed.

THE EDITOR'S CORNER

And what is so rare as a day in June?
Then, if ever, come perfect days . . .

With apologies to James Russell Lowell I believe we can add *and perfect reading, too, from LOVESWEPT and FANFARE . . .*

As fresh and beautiful as the rose in its title SAN ANTONIO ROSE, LOVESWEPT #474, by Fran Baker is a thrilling way to start your romance reading next month. Rafe Martinez betrayed Jeannie Crane, but her desire still burned for the only man she'd ever loved, the only man who'd ever made love to her. Rafe was back and admitting to her that her own father had driven him away. When he learned her secret, Rafe had a sure-fire way to get revenge . . . but would he? And could Jeannie ever find a way to tame the maverick who still drove her wild with ecstasy? This unforgettable love story will leave you breathless. . . .

Perfect in its powerful emotion is TOUGH GUY, SAVVY LADY, LOVESWEPT #475, by Charlotte Hughes. Charlotte tells a marvelous story of overwhelming love and stunning self-discovery in this tale of beautiful Honey Buchannan and Lucas McKay. Lucas smothered her with his love, sweetly dominating her life—and when she leaves he is distraught, but determined to win her back. Lucas has always hidden his own fears—he's a man who has pulled himself up by his boot straps to gain fortune and position—but to recapture the woman who is his life, he is going to have to change. TOUGH GUY, SAVVY LADY will touch you deeply . . . and joyfully.

Little could be so rare as being trapped IN A GOLDEN WEB, Courtney Henke's LOVESWEPT #476. Heroine Elizabeth Hammer is desperate! Framed for a crime she didn't commit, she's driven to actions she never dreamed she was capable of taking. And kidnapping gorgeous hunk Dexter Wolffe and forcing him to take her to Phoenix is just the start. Dex plays along—finding the beautiful bank manager the most delectable adversary he's ever encountered. He wants to kiss her defiant mouth and make her his prisoner . . . of love. You'll thrill to the romance of these two loners on the lam in one of LOVESWEPT's most delightful offerings ever!

And a dozen American beauties to Glenna McReynolds for her fabulously inventive OUTLAW CARSON, LOVESWEPT #478. We'll wager you've never run into a hero like Kit Carson before. Heroine Kristine Richards certainly hasn't. When the elusive, legendary Kit shows up at her university, Kristine can only wonder if he's a smuggler, a scholar—or a blessing from heaven, sent to shatter her senses. Kit is shocked by Kristine . . . for he had never believed before meeting her that there was any woman on earth who could arouse in him such fierce hunger . . . or such desperate jealousy. Both are burdened with secrets and wary of each other and have a long and difficult labyrinth to struggle through. But there are glimpses ahead of a Shangri-la just for them! As dramatic and surprising as a budding rose in winter, OUTLAW CARSON will enchant you!

Welcome to Tonya Wood who makes her debut with us with a real charmer in LOVESWEPT #477, GORGEOUS. Sam Christie was just too good-looking to be real. And too talented. And women were always throwing themselves at him. Well, until Mercy Rose Sullivan appeared in his life. When Mercy rescues Sam from the elevator in their apartment building, he can't believe what an endearing gypsy she is—or that she doesn't recognize him! Mercy is as feisty as she is guileless and puts up a terrific fight against Sam's long, slow, deep kisses. His fame is driving them apart just as love is bursting into full bloom . . . and it seems that only a miracle can bring these two dreamers together, where they belong. Sheer magical romance!

What is more perfect to read about on a perfect day than a long, lean, mean deputy sheriff and a lady locksmith who's been called to free him from the bed he is handcuffed to? Nothing! So run to pick-up your copy of SILVER BRACELETS, LOVE-SWEPT #479, by Sandra Chastain. You'll laugh and cry and root for these two unlikely lovers to get together. Sarah Wilson is as tenderhearted as they come. Asa Canyon is one rough, tough hombre who has always been determined to stay free of emotional entanglements. They taste ecstasy together . . . but is Sarah brave enough to risk loving such a man? And can Asa dare to believe that a woman will always be there for him? A romance as vivid and fresh and thrilling as a crimson rose!

And don't forget FANFARE next month with its irresistible longer fiction.

First, STORM WINDS by Iris Johansen. This thrilling, sweeping novel set against the turbulent times of the French Revolution continues with stories of those whose lives are touched by the fabled Wind Dancer. Two unforgettable pairs of lovers will have you singing the praises of Iris Johansen all summer long! DREAMS TO KEEP by Nomi Berger is a powerfully moving novel of a memorable and courageous woman, a survivor of the Warsaw ghetto, who defies all odds and builds a life and a fortune in America. But she is a woman who will risk everything for revenge on the man who condemned her family . . . until a love that is larger than life itself gives her a vision of a future of which she'd never dreamed. And all you LOVESWEPT readers will know you have to be sure to get a copy of MAGIC by Tami Hoag in which the fourth of the "fearsome foursome" gets a love for all time. This utterly enchanting love story shows off the best of Tami Hoag! Remember, FANFARE signals that something great is coming. . . .

Enjoy your perfect days to come with perfect reading from LOVESWEPT and FANFARE!

With every good wish,

Carolyn Nichols

Carolyn Nichols
Editor
LOVESWEPT
Bantam Books
666 Fifth Avenue
New York, NY 10103

THE LATEST IN BOOKS
AND AUDIO CASSETTES

Paperbacks

☐	28671	**NOBODY'S FAULT** Nancy Holmes	$5.95
☐	28412	**A SEASON OF SWANS** Celeste De Blasis	$5.95
☐	28354	**SEDUCTION** Amanda Quick	$4.50
☐	28594	**SURRENDER** Amanda Quick	$4.50
☐	28435	**WORLD OF DIFFERENCE** Leonia Blair	$5.95
☐	28416	**RIGHTFULLY MINE** Doris Mortman	$5.95
☐	27032	**FIRST BORN** Doris Mortman	$4.95
☐	27283	**BRAZEN VIRTUE** Nora Roberts	$4.50
☐	27891	**PEOPLE LIKE US** Dominick Dunne	$4.95
☐	27260	**WILD SWAN** Celeste De Blasis	$5.95
☐	25692	**SWAN'S CHANCE** Celeste De Blasis	$5.95
☐	27790	**A WOMAN OF SUBSTANCE** Barbara Taylor Bradford	$5.95

Audio

☐ **SEPTEMBER** by Rosamunde Pilcher
Performance by Lynn Redgrave
180 Mins. Double Cassette   45241-X $15.95

☐ **THE SHELL SEEKERS** by Rosamunde Pilcher
Performance by Lynn Redgrave
180 Mins. Double Cassette   48183-9 $14.95

☐ **COLD SASSY TREE** by Olive Ann Burns
Performance by Richard Thomas
180 Mins. Double Cassette   45166-9 $14.95

☐ **NOBODY'S FAULT** by Nancy Holmes
Performance by Geraldine James
180 Mins. Double Cassette   45250-9 $14.95

Bantam Books, Dept. FBS, 414 East Golf Road, Des Plaines, IL 60016

Please send me the items I have checked above. I am enclosing $_____
(please add $2.50 to cover postage and handling). Send check or money order,
no cash or C.O.D.s please. (Tape offer good in USA only.)

Mr/Ms _____

Address _____

City/State _____ Zip _____

FBS–1/91

Please allow four to six weeks for delivery.
Prices and availability subject to change without notice.

60 Minutes to a Better, More Beautiful You!

Now it's easier than ever to awaken your sensuality, stay slim forever—even make yourself irresistible. With Bantam's bestselling subliminal audio tapes, you're only 60 minutes away from a better, more beautiful you!

__	45004-2	**Slim Forever**	$8.95
__	45035-2	**Stop Smoking Forever**	$8.95
__	45022-0	**Positively Change Your Life**	$8.95
__	45041-7	**Stress Free Forever**	$8.95
__	45106-5	**Get a Good Night's Sleep**	$7.95
__	45094-8	**Improve Your Concentration**	$7.95
__	45172-3	**Develop A Perfect Memory**	$8.95

NEW!
Handsome Book Covers Specially Designed To Fit Loveswept Books

Our new French Calf Vinyl book covers come in a set of three great colors—royal blue, scarlet red and kachina green.

Each 7" × 9½" book cover has two deep vertical pockets, a handy sewn-in bookmark, and is soil and scratch resistant.

To order your set, use the form below.